Tangi stepped into the elevator and pressed the button for the fifth floor. The elevator stopped on the first floor for a passenger that made her heart descend into her stomach.

"John!"

Steele stared at the lone woman in the elevator. Her voice brought back memories that haunted him. "Jane?"

Tangi removed her glasses. "Yes, it's me."

Steele immediately pressed the stop button on the elevator control panel. He felt the same rush of passion he'd experienced in Porta Plataea. His eyes raked over her body with unbridled lust. He wanted to undress her, gaze at her exquisite figure, and make love to her.

But now was not the time. He was due in court in fifteen minutes.

BOOK YOUR PLACE ON OUR WEBSITE AND MAKE THE ARABESQUE ROMANCE CONNECTION!

We've created a customized website just for our very special Arabesque readers, where you can get the inside scoop on everything that's going on with Arabesque romance novels.

When you come online, you'll have the exciting opportunity to:

- View covers of upcoming books

- Learn about our future publishing schedule (listed by publication month and author)

- Find out when your favorite authors will be visiting a city near you

- Search for and order backlist books

- Check out author bios and background information

- Send e-mail to your favorite authors

- Join us in weekly chats with authors, readers and other guests

- Get writing guidelines

- AND MUCH MORE!

Visit our website at
http://www.arabesquebooks.com

THE BEST THING YET

Robin Allen

BET Publications, LLC
http://www.bet.com
http://www.arabesquebooks.com

ARABESQUE BOOKS are published by

BET Publications, LLC
c/o BET BOOKS
One BET Plaza
1900 W Place NE
Washington, DC 20018-1211

All Kensington Titles, Imprints, and Distributed Lines are available at special quantity discounts for bulk purchases for sales promotions, premiums, fund-raising, and educational or institutional use. Special book excerpts or customized printings can also be created to fit specific needs. For details, writed or phone the office of the Kensington special sales manager: Kensington Publishing Corp., 850 Third Avenue, New York, NY 10022, attn: Special Sales Department, Phone: 1-800-221-2647.

First Printing: October 2003
10 9 8 7 6 5 4 3 2 1

Printed in the United States of America

Dedicated to the readers who've sent me e-mails or letters. You're the fuel for my dreams.

One

Tangi Ellington didn't want to be supermodel Tangi Ellington. She just wanted to be Tangi. It's not that she didn't enjoy her career. In fact, she did. She loved the photo shoots and runway fashion shows. A rush of excitement coursed through her veins when she saw her face gracing magazine covers—each and every time. She didn't keep count of the number of magazine covers and photo shoots, but her niece did.

Jordy Peyton would periodically call Tangi to report the latest numbers. "It's my job to keep count," Jordy would proudly say about her self-appointed position. "You've been on forty-four magazine covers."

Tangi was living her dream in a way that exceeded her expectations. After three months of non-stop engagements, Tangi was physically exhausted and emotionally drained. It was a roller coaster lifestyle of super-size proportions—exciting, thrilling, exhilarating—but Tangi needed a reprieve. She needed to escape from the excitement of her life.

So, she headed to a place where she didn't have to worry about early morning wake-up calls, booking engagements, or the ever-intrusive paparazzi. A place where the only concern was deciding what to do for fun. A place where doing absolutely nothing was an accomplishment. A place where anonymity was the modus of operation.

That place was Porta Plataea, a spectacular resort on a private island in the Caribbean. The island was shaped like the heel of Italy and was only about seven miles long. There were golf courses, tennis courts, swimming pools, and the beautiful Caribbean splashing onto white sandy beaches. Fancy restaurants, boutiques, and jewelry stores abounded to suit a wide range of dining and shopping tastes.

Having traveled all over the world, Tangi was still taken by the beauty of the island, with so much color, foliage, and flowers to behold, including lush gardens that were perfectly manicured and maintained.

Porta Plataea was the picture of paradise. It could have served as the subject of a Pierre Renoir painting, offering beauty and tranquility.

Tangi luxuriated in the surrealism. The slow, easy pace of the day, the beauty of the island, the diamond-glistening beach, the balmy breeze, and the soothing lull of the night tides. She'd escaped from reality.

Her only connections to reality were the calls from her manager and agent. Initially, they were sympathetic to her request for rest. "Okay, you need a break." But when her break extended beyond four days, they became anxious and fretful.

"You're wasting time. Time is money," her agent said. "Ralph wants to book you."

Tangi hadn't planned to take an extended break.

But once she surrendered to the tranquility of the island and the taste of anonymity she wanted to enjoy the blissful existence a little bit longer—perhaps, a month or more. It would give her time to ponder her future and rejuvenate her soul. So, she stopped answering calls from her agent and manager. She did, however, answer calls from her family.

Tangi's reassurances to Romare Ellington that nothing was wrong didn't seem to register because her big brother still remained concerned. Sister-in-law Gillian Ellington immediately understood her need for peace, and encouraged her to take all the time she needed. Devon was supportive in his cool, laid back style: "I've been telling you for years that you work too hard. Chill time is long over due."

"It's really beautiful here. Do you want to come hang out with me?" Tangi asked, inviting Devon to join her.

"Thanks, but no thanks. I'm real busy. I have a lot of work to do."

"I still can't believe how much you've changed. You're all serious and focused."

"I finally found my calling," he said, laughing. "But this is your time, sis. Do nothing. Be still. Be at peace."

"Yes, and I'm staying away from men," she'd told Devon.

"Yeah, right," he said sarcastically.

"I'm serious."

"The question is: will men stay away from you?"

"I'll give them the evil eye," she joked, before ending their conversation.

Her career wasn't the only thing she was taking a

reprieve from. Two-legged creatures with an appendage between their legs were also on her get-away-from list: too much heartache, disappointment, and pain; not enough love, passion, and emotional fulfillment.

Tangi just wanted to be alone.

Lying in a lounge chair, her brown skin glistening with suntan lotion, Tangi's plans for the afternoon were simple: reading a book. A wide-brim straw hat and dark shades shielded her from the hot rays of the burning sun. She held a fruity drink in one hand and a book in the other.

Steele McDeal was thousands of miles away from home on a little-known island that transcended brochure descriptions and web site photographs—thousands of miles away from his penthouse apartment that had begun to feel claustrophobic; thousands of miles away from traffic, smog, and overcrowded streets; thousands of miles away from the symbolism and realism of American justice.

Steele McDeal was basking in the glory of his departure from New Orleans, Louisiana.

No gruesome cases to try.

No defense attorneys to battle.

No judges to defer to.

No disappointed victims to face when a "not guilty" verdict was read.

Just the peace and tranquility of days that began at noon and ended at midnight, the time in between unaccountable and unpredictable. To his employer, the New Orleans District Attorney's Office, he was absolutely incommunicado. Even to his family and friends, Steele was off-limits, with the exception of an emergency—a life and death type of emergency.

He was doing precisely what he wanted to do: sitting on a lounge chair, steps away from the beach, reading John Grisham's first legal thriller, *The Firm*. He had neither read the book nor seen the movie, too busy at the time pursing his own career in law. Even though he sought refuge from the real world of law and justice, he was inexplicably drawn to books with a legal theme. Mysteries, spy thrillers, and classic novels from Langston Hughes, Richard Wright, and Toni Morrison lined his bookshelves, along with books by and about painters and artists.

Turning the page, he pondered the main character's predicament. He knew the law firm's offer was too good to be true. It reminded him of the scene in *The Godfather*, in which Marlon Brando remarks: "We'll make him an offer he can't refuse." Perhaps it was his jaded experience as a prosecuting and tort attorney that made him suspicious. Perhaps it was his perceptions and insights into the dark side of human behavior. Or perhaps it was an intuitive foresight into the story's plot line. Still, he was engrossed and kept reading to find out if and how the character would save himself.

A sweet voice disturbed his concentration. It was soft and had a musical lilt laced with a slight Southern drawl. A non-Southerner probably wouldn't have detected it. Steele observed a tall, honeybrown woman standing at the bar. With her face hidden by a hat and glasses, he couldn't tell what she really looked like, but the outline of her face was extremely eye-catching.

"I'll have another one," the woman said.

"We would have brought it over to you, mademoiselle," the bartender responded in a French-accented voice.

She nodded. "Needed to stretch my legs."

"What book are you reading today?"

"*The Firm* by John Grisham. I think it was his first. "

"You're not the only one," the bartender said, sticking a straw with cherries into her drink.

Tangi took a quick survey of the vacationers' reading selections. She saw a plethora of reading tastes, ranging from fiction to non-fiction, from romance novels to biographies. She spotted a brown-skinned brother who was also reading *The Firm*. Smiling, he held up the book in a mock toast. She returned the smile and headed back toward her reading spot. Walking away, she felt his eyes on her. On impulse, she showcased her runway walk—sultry movements, exaggerated strides, hips swaying.

The sultry sway of her hips and rhythmic movement of her buttocks enraptured him. Steele couldn't view her face, but her body was ripe with temptation. Just watching her walk, more accurately, strut, stirred his desires. He shifted his legs, embarrassed that he'd responded to this woman in such a carnal way. It had been a long time since the sight of a woman went straight to his loins like a shot of liquor, leaving a burning sensation in its wake.

Steele watched her settle in her chair. She gazed at the ocean while sipping from her glass. After a while, she picked up her copy of *The Firm* and began to read.

Steele went back to reading *The Firm* also, but his concentration was not the same. Every other page, he'd look in her direction to see if she was still there.

After finishing a chapter, he decided to get a glass of water. Much to his disappointment, the woman with the sultry walk was gone.

Tangi returned to her suite with shopping bags filled with purchases for herself and gifts for her family. The phone was ringing when she unlocked the door. By the time she inserted the electronic key and entered the room, the ringing had stopped.

Tangi didn't care that she'd missed the call. She wanted to look at her purchases, especially the outfits she'd bought for her niece and nephew. Gillian and Romare would complain that she was spoiling Jordy and Nolan, but she'd ignore them as usual.

When the phone rang again, she picked up the receiver. "Hello."

"Having fun?" Devon asked.

"Yes. I'm all by my little self and I'm enjoying every moment."

"I can't believe you've been there for a week. And I can't believe your witch of a manager let you go."

Tangi laughed. Everyone complained about her no-nonsense agent. "Stop hating on Adele."

"She can be a real witch. I've seen her in action."

"I know. And that's why *I* don't have to be one."

"Oh, so she does all your dirty work," Devon said.

"That's one way of looking at it." Detecting something funny in his voice, Tangi asked, "So what's up?"

"I'm in trouble."

Her heart began to pound. "With the law? You been arrested?"

"No, nothing like that. I don't do anything to come under the police's radarscope. I don't speed. I don't drink and drive. You know how much I hate cops."

"So what kind of trouble are you talking about?"

A deep sigh echoed over the phone. "Financial."

"Financial? I thought you were rocking New Orleans with your web designs. Romare said you landed some big accounts. "

"That's partly true. Rick handles the sales and administrative stuff. Sometimes it takes a while for clients to pay."

"I'll sick Adele on your clients," Tangi teased, attempting to humor Devon into good spirits.

"I don't know whether to sick her on Rick or the accountants. My paycheck bounced. That's the second time it's happened."

"That doesn't sound right."

"I know. That's why I'm going to talk to Rick. I need to find out what the real deal is."

"I'll wire you some money, Devon," Tangi said. "That's no problem. But why didn't you ask Romare?"

"He's finally proud of me, and I don't want him to think I'm slipping."

"What's happening isn't your fault."

"I know. But I just want to handle things without always going to him for help."

"He wouldn't trip," she said.

"Yeah, yeah, but little sister's all banked up," he said, teasing her. "Got movie stars at her feet and—"

"Stop!" she lightly scolded Devon for teasing her about her celebrity status. She didn't take offense, it ws recurring banter. Her voice turned serious. "Sometimes it's just an illusion."

"For all I know, my company's so-called success might be an illusion. A different kind of illusion."

"I'll wire you the money in the morning, okay. Would ten thousand be enough?"

"I don't need ten G's."

"It'll be in your account tomorrow."

"Thank you, sis. Love you."

"Love you."

Steele departed from the elevator and moved in the direction of the jazz lounge. There were several lounges in the hotel, but a calypso singer was the featured guest of the Cashmere Bar for the evening, and Steele enjoyed calypso music.

His gaze caught a glimpse of familiar long legs and hips, moving with an erotic sultriness. As he did earlier that day, Steele watched the sway of her hips. He wondered if she looked as sexy as she walked. It wasn't long before he found out. She went and sat at an ocean-view table, not far from him.

She wasn't wearing glasses, nor was a hat hiding

her face. She did indeed look as sexy as she walked. Damn sexy.

Steele stared at her—unashamedly. He watched as she spoke with the waiter in an easy, friendly manner. When she caught him looking at her, he had no other choice. He had to introduce himself.

"Hello," Steele said as he leaned toward her. "May I join you for just a moment?"

Tangi quickly assessed him: a tall, handsome man with intelligent-looking eyes. She gave her consent.

"I saw you this afternoon," he said, sitting in the chair across from her. "You were reading *The Firm.*"

She smiled, magnifying her beauty. "I'm about a quarter into the story. I'm hooked. Can't wait to see how it ends."

"I think I know how it's going to end."

"You've already read it?"

Steele shook his head.

"You've seen the movie?"

"No."

"Well, I think the law firm is shady," Tangi said. "I can't believe the lawyers are the bad guys."

"It's not such a stretch to have lawyers acting like criminals."

"You must know something about the law."

"A little," he said, flashing a bright white smile. "So what brings you here?"

"I'm escaping from my life."

"Are you running away from something?"

"Nothing illegal. I'm running away from my busy schedule," Tangi said. "I needed a break or I was going to break."

"That's an interesting statement. Although I can identify with needing a rest from reality."

"So you're escaping too?" she probed.

"From the craziness of life," Steele said. "Are you enjoying this interlude?"

"Yes, indeed. This place is hakuna matata."

"Hakuna what?"

"Hakuna matata. It means no worries. It's a song from *The Lion King*. My four-year-old nephew is obsessed with the movie. He knows all the songs."

"I rarely watch cartoons." He paused to admire the sheer beauty of her face. His face didn't hide his thoughts, so he revealed them. "You are a very pretty woman." He spoke those words as if they made the difference between living and dying.

Tangi blushed. Magazines called her stunning, beautiful, glamorous, but for some strange reason, this man's simple compliment made her blush. It brought a strange tickle to the pit of her stomach that was different and wonderful. "Thank you."

"And you have a hell of a walk."

She laughed. "So I've been told," she said, realizing that he didn't know that she was a famous model. She was glad he didn't know.

"Husband, kids, boyfriends?"

"You're rather to the point. No, to all of the above."

"Why?"

"Another to the point question. I don't want to have kids until I'm married. I've never met anybody I wanted to marry. And my boyfriend was just a boyfriend, and he's no longer in my life."

"So you're not here to recover from a broken heart?" Steele asked.

"I wasn't in love."

"When was the last time you were in love?"

She smiled, then answered his question with a question. "When was the last time *you* were in love?"

"I've been so busy with work I haven't had too much time to focus on my heart," Steele said. "I'm just taking a much-needed vacation from my job."

"I can definitely relate to that," Tangi said.

"What job are you vacationing from?" Steele asked.

"I'd rather not say. I'm escaping from life and I just want to enjoy this moment in time."

"I understand," he simply said. "You want to be anonymous."

"I know it sounds strange and crazy, but this is paradise and the rules of life don't seem to apply here."

"So what shall I call you?"

"I don't know." A name from a movie script sent to her crept into her mind; she'd turned down the audition. She wasn't ready for such a dramatic role. Plus she still hadn't decided whether she wanted to venture into acting because she had a stronger interest in journalism. With a slight shrug, the name Jane came out of her mouth.

Steele's brows drew together. "As in Jane Doe?"

She giggled. "That's not what I was thinking, but I guess it works. So then, are you John?"

"John Doe?"

They both laughed.

Steele's face grew serious, as thoughts of cases with unidentified victims' names passed through his mind. Sometimes those cases couldn't be prosecuted. "You have no idea how ironic of a name."

"From the look on your face I don't think I want to know." She paused, not sure whether to continue the game. She saw him relax, then said, "Do I, John?"

Steele shook his head. "You don't."

The waiter arrived and placed a Caribbean seafood dish in front of Tangi.

"I guess that's my cue," Steele said. "Enjoy your evening . . . Jane."

Tangi raised her eyes to meet his probing gaze, sensing an erotic charge surging in their eye contact. She wondered if he felt what she had. "I will . . . John."

Two

It was noon. The sun stood in the middle of the cloudless blue sky. The diamond-glistening hot sand scattered around his sandal-clad feet as he walked along the beach searching for "Jane." Steele didn't think she would be difficult to find. There weren't many women of color on the island. A bevy of beautiful woman dotted the beach shoreline. Their beauty didn't compare to his mysterious Jane.

When he spotted her, he realized the name Jane was such an oxymoron. That name brought to mind the dowdy-looking woman in the television series *The Beverly Hillbillies* and the various women who played Jane in Tarzan movies. This Jane was no ordinary Jane.

He spotted her sitting along the beach reading. Her sexy walk captured his attention yesterday, but today it was her face. She didn't appear to have on any make-up, which accentuated her beauty. Her skin was flawless and her features were captivating—high slashing cheekbones, curvaceous lips, a narrow nose, and arched eyebrows over mesmerizing brown eyes.

"Jane!" Steele said to Tangi, but she didn't respond. He repeated her alias name, but she remained focused on the book in her hand. So, Steele tapped her shoulder.

The touch of his hand was that of a stranger, yet it felt oddly familiar. Tangi looked up from the exciting, plot-filled words on the page into the face of a man whose eyes promised excitement. His heavy, well-shaped brows almost met above the bridge of a long, straight nose. He had a strong, stubborn jaw line, and a deep cleft tucked inside his chin. His lips were firm, wide, and full. "Good morning, John."

"Good afternoon."

"It's after twelve?" she said, noticing his well-built frame, muscular thighs, and broad arms. She suspected he worked out on a regular basis. Yesterday she'd concluded that he was an unusually attractive man, but today she saw something different in his face: a sense of intelligence and character. He was a man who would be noticed and remembered.

"12:30."

"It's so easy to lose track of time here."

"This is the kind of place to get lost in time." He dropped into the empty lounge chair beside her. "How far along are you?" he asked, tapping the book in her hand.

"Tom is suspicious of the law firm. I think he's going to tell his wife."

"Now the plot thickens. Would you like to take a break from the book and go snorkeling?"

"Snorkeling?"

"See the beauty of the sea up close and personal."

"Swim with the fishes," she said in an unenthusiastic tone.

"You don't like swimming under the deep blue sea."

"The one and only time I went snorkeling . . . let's just say it wasn't a pleasant experience."

"What went wrong?"

"I couldn't get the breathing thing right."

"Breathing entirely through your mouth feels unnatural, but after you get the hang of breathing through a snorkel it becomes easier. The trick is not to bite down hard on the mouthpiece."

"I was biting on it for dear life."

"Relaxation is the key. Just inhale and exhale slowly and naturally."

"You make it sound easy."

"It'll be easy with me. I'll help you with your gear and everything."

"You'll stay with me?"

"Right beside you. I'm going with an experienced snorkeler. He's a native here and knows the water. He's actually taking a small group to a private area."

"It does sounds adventurous," she said.

He touched her arm, sending a shiver through her. "Are you in an adventurous mood?"

Tangi deliberated before answering. She was always receptive to new experiences. One bad snorkeling experience wasn't going to stop her from trying again. "I'm game."

"Meet me in the snorkel shop in a half-hour. I'll help you get your gear and then we'll go to the boat."

"I'll be there."

* * *

The only sound that could be heard was the roar of the boat's engine and the rush of the waves. All of the passengers were unusually quiet. There weren't any of the usual "Did you see that?" or "I've never seen anything like that before" remarks that are spoken after most tourist activities. It was as if the magnificence and wondrous beauty of the ocean had cast a spell. Spoken words would ruin the magic. The longer their silence, the longer they would feel the power and beauty of the experience.

It wasn't until the boat neared the marina that words were spoken. The tour guide's announcements about other snorkeling tours broke the spell, and everyone snapped out of the ocean's hypnotic trance.

"Did you enjoy yourself?" Steele asked when they departed from the boat. From the gleeful way she had smiled while in the water, pointing at the different fish, he already knew the answer to his question. Yet, he wanted to hear what she would say.

"It was fantastic! Out-of-the-world fantastic," Tangi exclaimed. "The fish, the reefs, the dolphins. It's the most Zen-like experience I've ever had. I would do it again in a heartbeat."

Hearing her unabashed pleasure filled his heart with joy. "I'm glad it was a better experience for you than last time."

"Thanks for helping me with my gear, especially showing me how to breathe. I think tour guides assume that if you're bold enough to put on the gear, then you must have done it before."

"Are you going to read your book?" he asked, standing near the ocean side of the dock as tourists moved past them.

She shook her head. "This is the perfect time for a nap."

"I'll probably take a nap after I've made some calls," Steele said.

"So you're going to let reality enter paradise."

"Just a little," he said, her smile making him redefine paradise. "But I think paradise is standing right before my eyes."

A hint of a smile formed on Tangi's lips. "I'll see you around."

"Enjoy your nap." He gently caressed her cheek, and then ran his fingers across her lips. Looking deep into her eyes, he said, "Maybe you'll dream of me."

"Maybe I'll dream of the deep blue sea." She didn't want to reveal that he'd been in her dreams the night before.

ICU patients are robbed of their dignity.

Spending five days in a hospital's intensive care unit had made Ruby DuBois intimately acquainted with humiliation. Between the powerful medication and the loss of physical and mental strength, she drifted in and out of consciousness. What Ruby despised most was feeling weak and powerless over her bodily functions.

With as much energy as her frail body could muster, she smiled wanly as the nurse changed I.V. bottles and inquired about her condition, hoping she could leave the ICU soon. The stern-faced nurse was curt in her answers. Ruby didn't particularly care for the woman with Blanche on her nametag. The nurse didn't have much compassion for patients. Ruby wondered if the woman was just plain cold and unfeeling or had the life and death nature of nursing hardened her heart. Her duties done, the nurse gave Ruby a patronizing smile and left the room. The room was silent except for the computerized machines monitoring her vital statistics, which beeped out their information on small green machines.

The nurse failed to answer Ruby's important questions: How long before she could leave? When could she go home? The biggest question she had was one that the nurse probably couldn't answer just yet: will she be able to go home and take care of herself?

Ruby closed her eyes to pray. *God please heal my body. Let me be able to take care of myself. I'm not ready to leave my children and grandchildren. Not just yet.*

"Mama! Mama!"

Before she opened her eyes she knew it was Mikey. It wasn't just the sound of his voice, but it was the stench of his breath. Liquor emanated from his body.

"You been drinking already," Ruby said, stretching her eyes to look at her only son, whose face mirrored the image of her long departed husband.

"No, Mama." Embarrassed, Mikey couldn't meet his mother's all-knowing gaze. "I was drinking last night."

"I worry about you, son. Why ain't you been to see me?"

"I ain't want to see you this way," he pointed to

the machines, "all hooked up to these here machines." He didn't want to tell her everyone told him to stay away from the hospital if he couldn't visit while sober.

"I'm going to get better, Mikey. Don't you worry."

"I really been wanting to see you, Mama. I been calling the hospital every day."

"You wanted to be sober," she said. Her voice was judgmental, but compassion shone in her eyes.

Mikey stared into his mother's face and realized she was too weak and sick to be angry. "I tried, Mama. I really tried."

"I know, son. You still working, right?"

"Yes, ma'am. I don't drink when I'm working."

"Just like your daddy."

"Gillian's coming later this afternoon. Aunt Mary and Aunt Lizzie will probably be here soon."

Ruby nodded. Her sisters visited her faithfully. "When is Jordy coming?"

"I don't know, Mama," he said, shrugging his shoulders. Suddenly, comprehension dawned on Mikey's face. "I think Jordy's afraid to come to the hospital."

Three

"I wouldn't if I were you."

Tangi turned in the direction of the commanding voice. She saw John Doe looking so distractingly handsome in his stark black evening clothes that she forgot what she was doing.

"Another card?" the Black Jack dealer asked Tangi.

She eyed the cards in her hand: two eights. Should she take the risk of adding another card? Would she get a five to score twenty-one? After a quick glance at John she said, "I'll hold."

The game was set in action as all players revealed their cards. The house's cards totaled twenty-three.

"Thanks," Tangi said to John when she didn't lose.

Steele slid into the chair next to her. "Mind if I play?"

"Of course not."

They played several games of Black Jack. Whether it was John's presence or the happenstance of luck, Tangi enjoyed a winning streak. The more she won, the more she played.

Steele watched her play enjoying her intense concentration and child-like glee upon winning.

Her laughter was infectious, revealing a zest for life that he found refreshing. She was friendly and warm to the other players who seemed to immediately like her.

She wore a sleek, black, sleeveless evening gown, held together at the waist by a single button, hidden by a large red silk flower. High-heeled black sandals drew attention to her legs and a pair of black bikini panties were her sole undergarment. The dress folded softly to the waist, showing the curve of her breasts quite clearly. Clearly enough for Steele to view and wonder what her brown nipples would taste like in his mouth.

She caught him staring at her breasts, then leaned over and whispered in his ear, "They're delicious."

"Reading my thoughts?" He raised an eyebrow, grinning unapologetically. "Or is my face that transparent?"

"Let's just say it's a familiar look."

"What's beauty if not to be admired?"

"My mother used to tell me that beauty is more than skin deep," Tangi said.

"Excuse me," the Black Jack dealer interrupted, "are you two playing?"

Steele and Tangi exchanged glances. Coincidentally, their thoughts were the same. "No."

"May I?" Steele asked, reaching for her hand.

A gentle smile was her consent.

"Let's go somewhere quiet." He took her hand and led her through the casino, to the outside deck that faced the ocean. They walked down the stairs to the lower patio and found a white-trellised gazebo. It was empty.

"So, tell me about yourself," Steele said, sitting across from her in the circular gazebo.

"Doesn't Jane Doe say it all?" she said, with girlish laughter. "Besides, I like the fact that we really don't know each other. "

"Tell me about yourself without telling me who you really are. Can you do that?

"Yes."

"I want to know about the inner you," he said, pausing for effect, "before I find out about the physical you."

She stretched her eyebrows. "You're that confident that you're going to experience the outer me."

Steele took her hand and placed a gentle kiss inside her palm. "You feel it, too, don't you?"

The question lingered in the air as if it were a statement of fact. Loud music drifted from the casino and mingled with the crushing roar of the ocean. And they just stared into each other's eyes under the star lit sky.

Several moments passed before Tangi answered his question. "I'm the baby in the family. My two older brothers have always been my protectors, especially when my parents died."

"How old were you when they died?"

"I was ten."

"So young. I'm sorry," he said, gently squeezing her hand. "What happened?"

"They were killed in a bus accident."

"What were your parents like?"

She gave him a curious look. No one had asked her that in a very long time. She closed her eyes to summon a picture of her father in her mind.

"Daddy was cool and fun to be with. He was tall and handsome and he was funny, kind of like Bill Cosby. He really loved my mama."

"He was a true blue kind of man," Steele said, reflecting on the fact that his father was the opposite. Although in reality he didn't know much about his father.

"My mother was the sweetest woman on this earth. Everybody liked her. She was carefree about most things, but very serious about education. She was a schoolteacher. I knew how to read when I went to kindergarten. The school wanted to put me in first grade, but my mother wouldn't agree to it. She didn't want me to grow up too fast, too soon."

"What happened when your parents died? Did you go live with your grandparents?"

"My big brother took care of me and D. . . my other brother. My big brother is thirteen years older than I am. He'd just finished grad school when my parents died. He had other plans, but he became our legal guardian."

"That was very noble and admirable."

"He didn't do it so that people would say things like that about him. I love him so much. He's my brother and like a father to me. He sacrificed his youth, so to speak, to take care of us. He never complained. Just handled his business as they say." She paused. "I do admire him. He worked hard and now he's a successful oil executive and he has a beautiful wife, who's like a big sister to me. I spoil my niece and nephew."

Steele didn't know her big brother, but he admired him as well. The tragedy of losing her parents at such a young age could have had a very negative impact. Had she not had this strong, heroic big brother, she might have turned to alcohol or drugs. But the woman before him was confident and sweet.

"What's the story on your other brother?"

"I'll call him D. He's crazy cool. It took him awhile to find himself. He went to two different colleges before he figured out what he wanted to do, but now he's a computer geek. He's Mr. Latest Technology. He taught me how to use a Palm Pilot and text message. It's funny now when he talks about his clients—he's all serious and focused. Before he was so lost. I'm proud of him, too. Very proud."

"Are they as proud of you as you are of them?"

She laughed. "Yes, they are. What can I say, we're a tight family."

"That's a beautiful thing. If more families were tight like that, the world would be better place. There'd be less crime," he said in a somber tone.

"Enough about me," Tangi said. "What's your life story?"

"You're the baby, but I'm the oldest. My mother raised me by herself until she married my stepfather. My siblings are twins, a boy and a girl. My sister got married a year ago and my brother is in grad school. The twins have completely opposite personalities, but they still have that twin thing going."

"I always wanted to be a twin."

"My Mom is what you'd call a tough cookie. She didn't marry my stepfather until I was eight or nine, and she worked hard to take care of us. I even went to Catholic school. When she married by stepfather, she softened. She didn't have to carry the load by herself. My stepdad is my hero. He coached me in football and kept me focused on school."

"So what about your biological father?"

"What about him?" he said with a defensive edge.

"Just a question, John Doe," she said.

"My dad is truly John Doe."

She gave him a curious look. "What do you mean?"

"I don't mean that I don't who my father is. I mean I don't know him. He's never been in my life. He's John Doe to me."

"Oh!" she said, his meaning clearer. "I'm sorry."

"He's actually a famous entertainer. If I said his name, you'd recognize it."

Even though she felt a flash of curiosity, she said, "You don't have to tell me who he is."

"Recently he's tried to make amends." Steele heaved a frustrated sigh. "But I haven't been very receptive."

"There's nothing you can do about the fact that he missed your childhood. You both have regrets, but that was yesterday. And you won't always have tomorrow to make amends. If you rebuild—"

"More like establish."

"Okay, if you establish a relationship now, you might discover something wonderful inside of you and inside of him. Something to be treasured, and you won't find it unless you open the door to the possibility."

"Are you a psychiatrist?"

"No," she said. "But, I did minor in psychology."

"You must be an old wise woman in disguise."

They became quiet, enjoying the cool ocean

breeze. They sat in silence for a while, but it wasn't an uncomfortable silence. Their thoughts were wrapped in the other's revelations. True experiences were shared, but not their true identities. At the moment, their personal identities didn't matter; it was what stirred in their hearts that mattered. But what that was, it was still undefined.

A kiss interrupted her thoughts when Steele leaned over and covered her mouth with his. The sensation of his lips was like a jolt of electricity, shocking and exciting. She felt another kind of heat. It spilled through her body, making her veins run as hot as rivers of lava. She couldn't remember ever feeling that way from a single kiss.

It wasn't just a simple kiss. Steele explored the softness of her mouth and felt the magnetic pull of her response. Instead of pulling away as his mind commanded, he kissed her deeper and deeper, feeling himself drawn to her passion.

When the kiss ended, they both were breathless and speechless.

Slowly, Tangi rose, feeling dazed. "Good night John," she managed to whisper before stepping out of the gazebo.

"Good night. Jane."

While searching for a parking spot, Devon Ellington scanned the lot for his business partner Rick Boullain's car. But the black jaguar wasn't in the restaurant parking lot. He was supposed to meet Rick at 11:30 A.M., before the lunch meeting with their potential clients at noon.

It was 11:35 A.M., so Devon picked up his cell

phone and called Rick. When Rick didn't answer, he called his girlfriend Brielle Mitchell. "Hey baby," he said, lowering the radio volume when she answered.

"Devon! I was just thinking about you," Brielle gushed into the phone.

He could feel the joy in her voice. "Were you thinking about last night?"

"I was thinking about this morning," she whispered.

"Ah, love the way you love me, baby," Devon said, singing the '70s disco song.

Brielle laughed. "Why do you like those old songs?"

"Maybe I have an old soul. Probably has something to do with the music my parents played back in the day."

"Back in the day," she said with much exaggeration. "So are you ready for your big meeting?"

"As ready as I'm going to be. But the problem is Rick. He isn't here yet. We were supposed to meet before the clients come so we can go over the proposal. We have to make sure we're singing the same song."

"He's probably on his way."

"He'd better be. I hate these kinds of meetings," Devon complained. "I'm not a salesmen. I just want to do the work."

"I hear you, baby, but the business world is—"

"Whack!" Checking out a Range Rover pulling into the lot, Devon groaned. "Damn! One of the clients just pulled up. Charlie Davis. He's a real talker. When he came to our offices, he wouldn't shut up. Rick better get here soon. I don't want to conduct the meeting without him. He put the proposal and the numbers together."

"Calm down," Brielle said. "Maybe he's running late."

"He hasn't called. He knows about the meeting."

"Has he ever not shown up for a client meeting?"

"No, but he's been acting strange lately." He started to tell her about the bounced payroll checks, but changed his mind. Their relationship was still too new to reveal details.

"If you had to, you could, right?" Brielle asked.

"I could what?"

"Run the meeting without him."

"I might have to." He consulted the dashboard clock. "It's 11:50 and Rick still isn't here."

"Maybe—"

"Now the other guy just pulled up," Devon said, banging his fist against the dashboard. "I vaguely remember the quote Rick wanted to propose."

"Go inside the restaurant," Brielle suggested. "Have lunch and by the time you get to the numbers, Rick will probably be there."

"I'm going to call Rick again, and then I'll go inside."

"You'll be fine," Brielle said, her voice brimming with confidence. "They're very interested or else you wouldn't be having this meeting, right?"

"True, true. I'll call you later."

Devon disconnected the call and stepped out of the car.

Four

Gillian Ellington immediately felt the change in temperature when she opened her car door—from sixty-six degrees inside the car to ninety-six degrees outside the car. By the time she left the parking lot, crossed the street, and stepped through the automatic doors into the air-conditioned lobby of St. Mercy's hospital, her clothes were clinging to her.

As she waited for the elevator, she checked herself in the mirrored wall and decided that she looked the way she felt—exhausted. She wore a leopard-print skirt and black tank-top. In the September heat, she didn't wear stockings, and low-heeled black sandals adorned her feet. Her blond-brown hair was styled in thin, long braids, a look she had recently adopted and still wasn't sure she liked.

What she saw in the mirror apparently was different from what Sydney Masterson had seen. An hour ago, she'd been at Xavier University, conducting a photo shoot of the school's board of directors. Along with formal shots of the directors, she was contracted to shoot photos of the staff, faculty, and students for use in the school's catalogs and brochures and on their web site. Gillian was surprised when the handsome vice president of finance boldly flirted with her. His initial comments were about her success as a freelance photographer. He touched her hand when he mentioned that he had a copy of her book, *The Age of Innocence*. At first she thought his friendliness was part of his professional demeanor, but then she noticed the glint in his eyes. His comments became more direct compliments about her face and figure. Somehow he managed to catch her alone, and he'd asked her to dinner.

Gillian was caught off guard. Most men respected the fact that she was a married woman with children. Some men would still flirt, but they knew they weren't being taken seriously, and soon they would stop. But Sydney Masterson was different. He didn't care that she was married, nor did it matter to him that she had no intention of being unfaithful to her husband. In fact, he'd even commented on her wedding ring.

"I'm not asking you to go to bed with me," Sydney had said. "I'm asking you to dinner. And dinner isn't being unfaithful."

"I'm not interested in having dinner with you," she'd firmly stated.

"Not just yet," Sydney said, a thin smile on his lips.

Gillian didn't like the way he looked at her. It wasn't a dejected I-tried-to-get-her look, but one of I'm-going-to-have-her determination.

Looking in the mirror, she couldn't imagine what she did to prompt him to outrageously flirt with her. Gillian wasn't exactly looking her best. She looked wilted, but everyone in sweltering, humid New Orleans looked wilted by the afternoon and drooped by evening time. She could blame the weather for her droopy appearance, but she couldn't blame the weather for the expression on her face. She hid her feelings while getting Nolan ready for school and dropping Jordy off at school. She put on her best professional face at the photo shoot. Neither the shoot crew nor the client knew the fear tumbling in her heart. Waiting for the elevator to take her to ICU, she no longer had a distraction from her heart's fear. She was inside the heart of her fear—in the hospital where her mother's heart was fighting to keep beating.

Gillian spotted her mother's doctor as soon as she stepped off the elevator. A short, balding man with wire-frame glasses was standing in front of the nurse's station, his attention on a patient chart. She walked over, spoke to the nurses, and then said, "Hello, Dr. Nichols."

"Mrs. Ellington, how are you today?"

"Fine. Just tired."

"Photo shoot today?" He pushed his glasses against the bridge of his nose.

"A long one. So, how's my mother?"

"Basically the same," he said, taking the chart from a nurse. It was Ruby DuBois' chart.

"Is that good or bad?" she asked, frowning with worry.

"Rather not have a change for the worse." Dr. Nichols flipped open the chart.

"Of course not."

"Your mother's definitely going to need bypass surgery. Maybe a triple bypass."

Gillian ran a hand through her tangled mass of

braids. This wasn't good news. The doctor had warned her of the possibility of surgery. "When?"

"She isn't strong enough yet. We have to wait until she builds up her strength."

"Is that what the cardiologist recommends?"

"Yes."

"Okay. What can you do to help her get strong?"

"Let her rest and give her body time to recover from the heart attack."

"How much time?"

"We're hoping within the week."

"Will she be in ICU?"

"Probably." He looked at Ruby's chart for a minute, then said, "But if she starts to improve, we'll move her to a regular room, give her a couple of days to build up her strength on her own, and then we'll perform the bypass. That's the optimal way to go."

Gillian slowly nodded. "I was hoping to bring my niece to see her."

"How old is she?"

"She's eleven."

"She's really too young for ICU, but I can make an exception if you think she's mature enough to handle it."

"I don't know. Her mother, my sister, died in a hospital when she was six. She didn't see her in the hospital or anything, but all she knows is that her mother died in a hospital. Needless to say, she doesn't like hospitals."

"I understand, Mrs. Ellington. If your mother's condition improves and we move her out of ICU before the surgery, your niece can see her then."

"That sounds like a good idea," Gillian said.

"What's the probability that she'll be moved before the surgery?"

Dr. Nichols pondered the question before answering. "Probably 60-40."

Steele awakened with a woman on his mind—a mysterious woman named Jane: the graceful way she moved; the feminine gestures she unconsciously made with her slender hands; the long legs and delicate feet; the expressive movements of her brown eyes; and all that wavy black hair.

It'd been a long time since a woman lingered in his mind longer than a gust of wind—here and gone, and then forgotten. But Jane's presence was like a careless whisper that invaded his mind with non-stop wonder. Who was she really? Where did she come from? How can she afford to stay in this expensive resort?

For a moment, he wondered if she was running from the law—a black widow spider woman who killed her husband for money. Maybe she poisoned her husband, collected the insurance money, and married again, repeating her crime. The death of her second husband roused suspicions about her first husband's death. An investigation was launched and both husbands' bodies were exhumed. An autopsy revealed that they'd both been poisoned by anti-freeze. So, she fled to a place where there weren't extradition laws.

Steele shook his head, dismissing that thought. Jane was too sweet and guileless to be so heartless and utterly ruthless.

Remembering a news article about an international counterfeit ring, he considered the possibility that she was the ringleader's woman who had never been identified by government authorities.

She certainly fit the profile. Criminal ringleaders were known to have beautiful women, as if the woman's beauty deflected the ugliness of their criminal activity.

But Steele cast that thought from his mind. He chided himself for his suspicious view of people, courtesy of his profession as a prosecuting attorney. She was too genuine to be engaged—directly or indirectly—in criminal activity.

He wondered if she was an actress or maybe she'd been married to a professional athlete. But then he remembered that she'd never been married. He concluded that he would have recognized her if she were an actress or a celebrity. Besides, he was never attracted to celebrities. They were too self-centered and arrogant, and Jane was too down-to-earth and didn't have an I'm-a-diva attitude.

The possibility that she was a celebrity didn't take root because she didn't act like one. Plus, Steele disliked celebrities. His disdain came from having a famous father, a member of the famous singing group *The Vibrations,* whose records were big hits in the '60s and '70s. Jeremy Benson had a brief love affair with his mother Camille McDeal. She was young and impressionable, and believed Jeremy's promise of ever-lasting love. But when Camille discovered that she was pregnant, Jeremy stopped visiting her when he came to town. He never questioned that he had fathered her child, but he didn't want to fulfill the responsibilities of a father. He didn't have time. So, he periodically sent Camille checks—nothing that she could count on, forcing her to find a way to take care of herself and Steele.

At the moment, Steele didn't know who Jane really was, and that was part of the game they were playing, and he was enjoying the game. After all, they were on a beautiful island, far away from the real world. Did who they really were matter?

Point of fact, Steele was more interested in getting Jane into bed than uncovering her real identity. He wanted to do more than kiss her. He wanted to wrap his mouth around the fullness of her breasts. He wanted to see her naked body. He wanted to have mad, wild sex with her.

Getting out of bed, he decided that he would pursue her until he got her into bed. After they returned to the realities of their lives, it wouldn't matter who they each were.

Eyes closed, Tangi let herself float away into the physical sensations her body was feeling from the administrations of the masseur. His hands were kneading the deep tissues of her shoulder muscles. She drifted in and out of sleep while imagining how it would feel if John's hands and mouth were touching her body. The way he lustfully looked at her breasts, she could only imagine how it would feel if his mouth introduced itself to her nipples: swirls of indescribable pleasure. If his kiss was any indication of his love making abilities, she'd never want to leave this island.

When the masseur directed Tangi to turn onto

her back, her thoughts spun in a different direction. She reminded herself that she'd come to Porta Plataea not only to ponder her future, but also to escape from men, especially men who pretended to be something they really weren't. Case in point: Brock Wilson, her last boyfriend, who assumed the identity of an investment broker. He had lavished attention on her in a devout fashion. Brock called her every day, and ingratiated himself into her life. Maybe it was intuition or self-protecting suspicion, but she didn't allow herself to fall in love with him. So when she found out he was the son of an investment broker and unemployed, she was disappointed, but not devastated by his deception.

But it also left her feeling empty—intensifying the emptiness that was always there but cloaked by the glamour of her lifestyle. Relationships masqueraded as love. The realization that she'd never really fallen in love saddened her. Was it because of her celebrity life? Did she keep her heart too closely guarded? Had she simply not met the man who could make her feel something inside her heart?

She hadn't discovered the answers to these questions in this retreat from reality. But what she had discovered was a longing for something more. For reasons unknown to herself, she thought about John—the mysterious John Doe. They were playing a charade-like game. It intrigued her, igniting something inside her soul. Maybe that's why his kiss made her feel like the sun singed her.

"Mademoiselle," the masseur interrupted Tangi's thoughts. "Au fini."

"Okay," she said, slowly opening her eyes.

"You should be totally relaxed. I did a deep tissue massage," the blond-haired masseur said with a lyrical French accent. "I hope you are satisfied."

"I'm satisfied," Tangi said, raising up from the massage table. "And I'm sleepy."

"Why don't you go back to your room and take a nap," the masseur suggested.

"That's exactly what I plan to do. I don't have any energy to do much else."

"Good day, mademoiselle," the masseur said before leaving the small room.

Tangi slipped on her shorts and a T-shirt, and went into the massage salon's small waiting room. Her hand was wrapped around the door knob when the masseur tapped her shoulder.

"Pardon moi, I forgot to give you this." He handed Tangi a square-shaped envelope. "This tall, very handsome gentlemen brought it by. He had lust in his eyes for you," he said flirtatiously.

Tangi stared at the envelope. The name Jane was handwritten across the front. There was a certain elegance to the penmanship. She looked at the masseur. "Thank you."

"Oui, oui, you have lust for him. I just saw it," he said.

A blushing smile was her reply.

"That's a good thing you know. When the same two people have lust for each other." He shook his head. "Not a good thing when the person you lust for doesn't lust for you."

"How so very true," she said, then opened the door and left the massage salon.

She couldn't wait to read the note, so she tore the seal while standing in the hall. It read:

Jane,
   Please join me for dinner this evening. 8:00 at the
Baja Restaurant.
                                                      John

Five

It was eight o'clock in the evening. The night was perfectly clear, the stars bright points of light overhead, and the air sweet and pungent from the mingling flowery scents and the salty tang of the Caribbean.

It was the perfect evening to fall in love, Tangi thought as she entered the restaurant. When the maitre d' escorted her to John's table, she realized how incomplete that thought was. He—the mysterious John—was the perfect man to fall in love with. Very well-dressed in a cool white linen suit, his hair was smoothed back in dark waves.

Watching her approach, Steele wondered if he would ever want to return to reality. Why couldn't moments in time be infinitely suspended? He wanted to savor the moment for more than a wisp of time—a beautiful woman dressed in a scandalously revealing red dress, strutting seductively toward him as if he were the king of Egypt. Her hair was piled on top of her head with tendrils floating about her face. This woman had somehow gotten underneath his skin—and he didn't even know her real name. But that was the fun of it, wasn't it?

"Good evening, Jane," he said, rising from the table. "You look absolutely delicious."

Tangi blushed. "And I'm not even the main course."

"Dessert, perhaps?" Steele gestured to the menu. "I thought I saw Crème de la Jane on the dessert menu."

A radiant smile spread across Tangi's red-stained lips.

"I can have the chef prepare it if you tell me the main ingredients," the maitre d' offered.

Merriment danced in Steele and Tangi's eyes as laughter erupted from both their lips.

"Forgive me, I understand now," the maitre d' said, upon realizing that they were outrageously flirting with each other. "We can still accommodate special requests." Not to be outdone, he added, "But not the kind requiring human body parts."

He granted them a smile, while placing menus in front of them. "Peruse the menu and the waiter will be with you shortly."

Settled back in his chair, his eyes focused on Tangi, he said, "Perhaps I should amend my compliment. You look stunning. Runway model stunning."

Tangi elongated an eyebrow, wondering if he'd found out who she really was.

"That was a compliment," Steele explained when his comment elicited a cautious stare.

She nodded. "And you are rakishly handsome."

"Rakishly?"

"That was a compliment," she said, replaying his words to her.

They were laughing when the waiter arrived with a bottle of champagne.

"I ordered it before you arrived."

"Shall I?" the waiter asked, the opened champagne bottle poised over Tangi's crystal-rimmed goblet.

"Certainly."

The waiter poured champagne in both goblets, then departed from the table.

Steele raised his glass. "A toast. To the sun, the sand, and the pursuit of prurient—"

"Are you a lawyer or something?" she quipped. "How about to fantasies and . . . fetishes."

"How apropos." He tapped his glass against hers. "You must tell me yours."

"Only if you tell me yours."

Steele watched her bring the goblet to her lips. Lips he wanted to kiss.

The champagne was tart on Tangi's tongue, but it was bubbly and cold as she sipped it.

"I'll reveal one of my fantasies," he said, thoroughly enjoying the direction of their conversation.

"You have many?" she probed.

He cocked an eyebrow, a sexy grin on his face.

"Well, what's your fantasy?" Tangi asked.

"Meeting you."

"Am I supposed to say that meeting you is my fantasy?" she asked, realizing there were elements of truth in that question.

The question hung in the air before Steele finally said, "Only if you feel that way . . . Jane."

"Free is how I feel right now, John." Tangi leaned her head back and released a burst of laughter. "Free from the responsibilities of my everyday life."

"Somehow I get the feeling your life isn't so bad," Steele said.

"It's a wonderful life," she said, nodding her head. "It's exciting and fun and very chaotic." Her voice turned serious. "And sometimes unfulfilling."

"I can relate," he said. "I came here partly to rediscover the meaning of life. What I deal with sometimes is so dark and jaded, it can be mind-boggling."

"No, no, no! You're going to give yourself away," she said, swishing her hand back and forth. But, she couldn't resist the bait. "It sounds like you're a doctor or a psychologist. You deal with the human psyche in a way that's frightening."

"That's an interesting interpretation." Steele sipped the champagne. "Admit it, you're just as curious about the real me as I'm curious about the real you."

"Maybe I am," she said with a slight shrug. "But then it would destroy the fantasy and I'm enjoying the fantasy too much."

"So am I." He paused to scan the menu and behold the ocean view. "In your real life, are you living your dream in some way?"

"What do you mean?"

"You know how when you're a child you say, 'I want to be a teacher or a fireman when I grow up.' Are you living the dreams of your childhood?"

Runway shows, flashing lights, and photo shoots popped in Tangi's head. As a child, she simply dreamed of being a model. She had no idea what that lifestyle really meant. Her life, in many ways, was a dream. "My life is way beyond what I dreamed. Much bigger than I imagined. I guess you don't know what something's like until you experience it."

"Like sex," Steele said. "No one can tell you what it feels like. You have to experience it to know how it feels."

She gave him a befuddled look. "I don't think that connects to what I just said."

"It connects to what I'm thinking. But we'll get to that."

"Maybe," she said, leaning forward, knowing that movement revealed more than a hint of her breasts. She saw him feast upon her cleavage with his eyes, then stare into her face, lust undisguised. "Are you living your childhood dream?"

He tilted his head. "Too bad you can't try out your dream before you try to live it."

Brows knit together, she remarked, "Can you be any more obscure?"

He laughed at her repartee. "Let's say you want to be a fireman, which by the way I never wanted to be. Anyway, you train to be a fireman because you get to be a hero and save people's lives. You put out your first fire and get to go inside a burning building. But then you realize that fire scares the hell out of you. Your dream job, your fantasy of being a hero, collides with reality."

"Somehow, you're telling me that you pursued a career, discovered you didn't like it, and changed careers."

"Let's just say I found another area where I could apply my expertise," he obliquely explained, referring to his five-year stint as a tort lawyer. He had won many cases and made a lot of money. But there was no thrill in it; tort law completely bored him.

He considered becoming a defense attorney, but decided to become a prosecuting attorney. It made no sense to his family and friends when he took a significant pay cut to enter the jungle fields of criminal justice. He lost his fiancée at the time, but he got back his dream.

"Do you like it better?"

"Some things are better in a bottle. To observe and wonder."

"Which means?"

"Some days I like what I do and some days I don't. The core of what I do I really love." He paused, a contemplative look on his face. "I have a hobby that takes me away from my real world to a world that I create."

"What kind of world?" she asked, curiosity framing her features.

"I'm an artist. I like to paint."

"Really?"

"It's just a hobby. I don't make a living at it. There was a time when I imagined myself to be a Jacob Lawrence or a Romare—"

"Bearden."

"So you're familiar with him. I haven't painted in years, but this place, with all this beauty, makes me want to pull out my paint brushes," he said.

"So you're not here to find a new dream?"

"No," he said, a gentle look on his face, "but you are."

"I came here to reflect and decide how I want to change my life. My mother, I think she must have been a visionary or something, used to tell me that life is full of many choices." She paused to ponder an old memory. "She didn't tell me I had to do just one thing. She told me that I have many talents to pluck from. As a kid, her words were contrary to what everyone else said. My teachers used to tell me that one day I would have to choose one career. But now, I realize that I can be many things in my life."

"My mother always talked about how short life is. Her favorite quote from the Bible is some reference to time in a blink of an eye." He shrugged his shoulders, a thoughtful expression on his face. "So, I've always had a sense of urgency about life. I graduated from high school in three years. I was in such a hurry to be an adult."

"Me too." She touched his hand, her eyes glinting in amusement. "I used to complain to my brother that I couldn't wait to graduate from high school." She smiled and softly said, "I was in a hurry to get to my dream."

"And now?"

"That is the question of my life. The now what?"

"And this time you're taking your time."

"I guess I am. My next dream can wait." She looked deeply into his eyes. "Right now, I just want to enjoy my fantasy."

Gillian pressed the automatic garage door opener and drove her Lincoln Navigator inside the three-car garage. She grabbed some shopping bags and got out of her SUV. She opened the door leading into the kitchen and was greeted by silence. She'd expected to find Romare dozing on the sofa, Nolan's head resting on his lap, the TV blasting. But the house was as silent as a mouse.

She was relieved to find the kitchen tidy and

shiny. It was after ten P.M. and she didn't feel like cleaning, but if she had to, she would, because she hated waking up to a dirty kitchen. She peeked inside the wide stainless-steel refrigerator, but didn't see anything she wanted to eat. She noticed a covered dish on the table with a plate of baked chicken, rice, and green beans. Too much food before bedtime, so she put the plate in the refrigerator.

Yawning, Gillian climbed the back stairs to the upper level. She opened Nolan's bedroom door, and expected to find his bed empty. But Nolan was asleep in his sports-decorated bedroom, and not in bed with Romare. She lovingly stroked his forehead, a maternal smile on her face from the joy in her heart. Her son was a very special boy: handsome, bright, funny. She shook her head upon seeing her book, *The Age of Innocence*, on the floor near his bed. Nolan loved the photos in the book; he'd point and laugh at the expressions on the kids' faces.

Still so innocent, she thought, kissing him on the forehead.

She found Jordy asleep in her bed, her covers wildly twisted and her opened social studies book lying next to her. Closing the book and placing it on the dresser, Gillian remembered that Jordy had a social studies test the next day. She straightened the covers and kissed Jordy before leaving the room.

Expecting Romare to be asleep like everyone else, Gillian wasn't prepared for the array of candles burning in the master bedroom. The aroma of cinnamon and jasmine filtered the air.

"Hey, baby," Romare said from the leather chair.

"Romare, I thought you were asleep."

"You know I can't really go to sleep if you're out late."

"That's why I was surprised to find the house locked up," she said, hugging him. "Thank you for taking care of dinner and cleaning up the kitchen."

"I know you had a long day."

"Too long," she said, releasing a heavy sigh. Turning toward the master bathroom, she saw that the jacuzzi tub was filled with bubbles. "You ran me a bath!" She went back over to the open sitting room adjoining the master bedroom. "You're the sweetest man on this earth." She kissed him several times on the lips.

"Enjoy your bath. I'll wait up for you."

Poised in the doorway of the bathroom, "Or you can join me, if you like," she said, in a seductive voice.

He shook his head. "I'll give you time to relax and unwind."

"How did your meeting go with Harry?"

"Fine. He's worried about the numbers, but everyone is. We have to ride out the economic storm," he said, while watching her undress. "Jordy really wants to see your mom. She mentioned it at dinner."

"I know she does. The doctors hope they can move Mama out of ICU for a few days before they operate," Gillian explained. "He says it's a 60-40 chance that they'll move her, then Jordy can visit her. I'm just not sure if I should make Jordy wait."

"She really wants to see her, and I think she's ready. I know she hates hospitals, but in the back of her mind, I think she's afraid that she won't see Mama Ruby before something goes wrong."

"Just like with Nolah," Gillian said, thinking about the fateful night when she lost her big sister, and, ironically, found Romare. "I'll talk to her about it."

"Devon called a little while ago. He wanted to talk to you about using some of your photo images from . . ." he paused, "I forgot what shoot. Anyway he wants to use some pictures for a web site he's designing."

"I'll call him tomorrow."

"He sounded strange when I inquired about the business. He made a rather derogatory statement about Rick's business practices."

"Really," Gillian said, forcing herself to sound surprised. Devon had discussed his concerns with her about his partner, but had asked her not to tell Romare. He'd told her: "I don't want Romare thinking I'm out of my league, that I can't handle my business."

"Have you heard from Tangi?" Romare asked.

"She hasn't called. She's probably having a wonderful time."

"That's what *we* need to do. When things calm down, let's go somewhere special," Romare said. "Just the two of us."

"I'd love to," Gillian said, sliding into the hot water and immediately feeling the tensions of the day melt away. She eased her head against the pillow rest and willed her mind to be still. She didn't want to think about today or the decisions facing her tomorrow. She just wanted to be still, and find the source of her strength.

She fell into a light sleep, waking up when the water temperature had cooled and the bubbles dissipated. She emerged from the tub and dried herself with a thick, king-sized towel. She poured scented lotion all over her body, smoothing it into her moist skin. She wrapped the towel around her, and went into the bedroom to retrieve a nightgown.

She reached for the gown on the bed, but Romare pulled it away from her grasp.

"You won't be needing that," he stated simply, his voice dark with desire.

Gillian felt the pull of his passion, the pulse of his desire. It was after midnight when she slid her naked body under the covers next to her husband. Another hour would pass before she'd actually be asleep. But she didn't care as Romare's fingers caressed her breasts and stroked the tenderness of her thighs. It would be the best hour of her day.

Six

Rick Boullain had a pleasant buzz going when he left the Bourbon Street bar. He wasn't staggering, nor was he lucid enough to effortlessly insert his key into the car lock. He fumbled and dropped his keys, and after several attempts to insert the key into the lock, finally opened the door.

Behind the car wheel, he forced himself to concentrate on the tasks at hand: finding his cell phone and driving home. A quick search of the passenger seat revealed the phone. He picked it up and said "voicemail," activating the voice command feature. Seconds later he was listening to his messages.

There were two messages from Devon: "What's up with the finances? Hit me back," then "Don't dis me, man! I want to know what's going on."

Then there were three messages from his bookie: "When are you going pay those ten Gs?" "I want my money now!" "Don't make me come looking for you! Your daddy can't get you out this one."

All four messages from Isadora Graham were the same: "I want to see you. Can I come over?"

Rick called Isadora back.

"I want you now."

"Hold on, sugar. You can't say, 'Hello, Isadora, how are you? How's your day?'"

"I'm not in the mood for conversation," Rick tersely said.

"Still in a financial pickle?"

"I said I'm not in the mood to talk," he said gruffly, regretful that he'd confided in her about the tangled morass of his financial affairs.

"Sugar, why don't you get the money from your daddy. Richard's a very generous man."

"What do you know about him?" he asked, slamming on the brakes at a red light.

"Sugar, everybody knows your daddy is as free with money as a whore on Bourbon Street is with sex."

"Sex, that's what I want. Meet me at my apartment."

"Why don't you come here?" she asked in a honey-coated voice.

"I've been drinking and I shouldn't be driving now." He eyed the speedometer to make sure he was staying within the speed limit. "There's no way I can drive over to your place."

"You know drinking and driving is against the law."

"What I want to do to you is against the law. Now get your pretty little ass to my place."

"Sugar, I didn't hear you say please."

Several moments passed before Rick finally said, "Please, Isadora."

"I'll be there before you can say, 'Oh baby, that feels so good.'"

* * *

Sex was on Steele's mind. Sex had been on his mind all night, waking him up from a restless sleep, his thoughts on Jane. He wanted to have sex with her. It didn't matter who she was. It didn't matter where she came from. He wanted to be with her, talk with her, laugh with her, and play their don't-tell-me-your-name game.

If only he could find her.

He'd spent the day looking for her. It crossed his mind to inquire about her at the front desk, but suspected they wouldn't tell him where or who she was because anonymity was one of the resort's key selling points. Knowing her real identity would ruin the game, and he was enjoying the game too much. But now it was time to take the game to another level. When he considered the possibility that she'd left the resort, his heart stopped beating. He quickly dismissed that possibility, convincing himself that she was enjoying their little game too much to leave.

But where was she?

He took a seat in the jazz club. Sipping on a drink as jazz played in the background, he recalled their conversation over dinner. To the casual observer, he was relaxing in the cool breeze and enjoying the hot sounds of the alto sax. But Steele had chosen that particular seat for a reason. He was watching everyone who went through the lobby.

A pair of hips went sashaying by. That erotic walk. He watched her take a seat on the patio and order a drink before he approached her.

"Beautiful night."

His voice accelerated her heart rate. Tangi

leaned her head back to view the sky. "Very beautiful."

"I've been looking for you," he said, joining her at the table.

"You have?"

"Have you been hiding?" he asked, a crooked smile on his face.

A moment passed before she said, "I've been very busy."

"I've been very busy," he said, "busy thinking about you, Jane."

"What have you been thinking?"

"Where this fantasy should lead."

"And where is that?"

"Between the sheets."

She studied his face for a long time. She knew this moment would come. She wanted it to come. She'd been waiting for it all day. "Yours or mine?"

"Mine."

"If you came into my room you would know who I am." Then she hesitated before saying, "I've never been what you call easy. I don't sleep around and I've never slept with a stranger."

"We're not total strangers. We've shared a lot about each other."

"That's true," she said. "Everything but the fine details."

"I'll tell you who I am," he said, shrugging his shoulders.

She leaned over and put a finger over his lips. He clasped her hand, then kissed her fingers, one by one, sending a chill over her. "That would ruin the fun."

"The fun has just begun. . . . Follow me."

They made their way to Steele's room, kissing in the elevator and the hallway along the way. Inside his room, he turned on the lights, and then she turned them back off.

"I want to see what you look like," he said.

She slowly bobbed her head up and down.

Steele turned on the bedside lamp, then moved back to where Tangi stood near the door.

"I want to undress you," he said, untying the halter straps of her dress and slowly gliding the dress down her frame. He stared at her brown-tipped breasts before running his fingers across her nipples. He pulled the dress down to the floor and was stunned to discover that she was pantiless. His manhood bulged inside his pants.

"You don't wear panties in a dress like this," she explained.

"I guess not. You are absolutely beautiful."

"Thank you."

"Can I ask you to do one thing?"

"Nothing kinky."

"Just walk for me. I don't know where you got that walk from but it does something to me."

She laughed, realizing that he didn't have any idea that she was a model. "Do you have condoms?"

He nodded.

She became serious. She didn't want to have sex with a total stranger. "What's your middle name?"

"Jeremy."

"My middle name is Noelle."

A long moment passed before Tangi began to strut around the room, moving her hips as she did down the fashion runway.

The second time she paraded across the room,

he met her halfway. "I can't wait anymore," he uttered, pushing her against the wall, then placing his hands around her face, pressing his lips against hers. They engaged in an orgy of kissing, carnal and dark.

When he stopped kissing her lips, he ran his open mouth against her neck. He flicked her earlobe with his tongue. "You are the sexiest woman I have ever seen," he growled while taking her hands and holding them firmly against the wall. "Don't move."

It was a command, but Tangi didn't object to his tone. It was a command that promised ecstasy.

He swept her mouth with his tongue before taking a nipple into his mouth, going back and forth in a slow, sensual motion.

A low groan escaped her mouth when he grabbed her breast with his lips, teasing her nipple with his tongue. "I like your breasts. Your nipples are brown and full. I like how they feel inside my mouth. Delicious."

She wanted to move, but couldn't. His hands had her gently pinned against the wall. When he wasn't talking seductively, his mouth was acting seductive.

"How will you taste . . . inside there," he said, his fingers rubbing against her wet flesh. He found her moist, sensitive spot and stroked it with his fingers.

Tangi had never had a man do this to her before, and she'd never felt anything like it in her life. Backed against the wall, her body was on fire.

His fingers rubbed the inside of her. "You're so wet and warm." He kissed her mouth, so intense it was savage. "I bet you taste so sweet . . . there."

His fingers were sliding over her, pushing downward to touch her and it was the most intense feeling she had ever had. The anticipation of what it would feel like when he tasted her weakened her with moist desire.

The palm of his thumb wiggled inside her. "I think I'll find out now."

The moment of contact—his tongue touching there—felt like an explosion of astronomical sensations. He drew the silky, slippery softness between his lips.

"I was right. You taste sweet," he said as he kept his mouth between her legs.

Tangi tried to move but couldn't. He held her arms firmly against the wall.

"Don't move. It's just going to get better," he promised.

It did get better and better, his tongue taking her to an unfamiliar level of passion.

"You taste so good," he said, using his flicking, stroking, questing tongue to bring her to one crashing climax after another.

He released her arms, and then she felt him plant tender kisses along her neck.

"Oh, oh, oh," she moaned breathlessly. Realizing that she was naked and he was still fully dressed, her face reflected confusion and embarrassment.

"It's okay, baby," he soothingly said, taking his clothes off while leading her to the bed.

"We've only just begun."

Seven

Tangi returned to her room the next morning feeling tired, sleepy, and hungry. But she was sexually satiated. She felt good—damn good.

For the first time since arriving at the Port Plataea Resort, she made plans for the day: play tennis with John. First she had to shower, eat, and take a nap.

Three hours later, she met John at the tennis courts. Walking towards him, she had a flashback of their sexual encounter, an erotic encounter that made her feel like she had had an out of body experience. The flashback brought back swirling sensations of desire. It took a concentrated effort to push those sensations out of her mind, but they only returned when Steele greeted her with a kiss, sliding his tongue inside her mouth.

"Good afternoon . . . Jane."

A slow, sexy smile curved her lips. "Kiss me like that again and we won't be playing tennis."

"Is that a threat?"

She returned his passion-filled gaze. "And this time you'll be the one with your back against the wall."

He ran his finger across her cheek. "That's the kind of threat I like."

Sexual tension hung in the air.

"Let's play," she said, picking up a rented tennis racket. She moved around to the other side of the court. Standing near the net, she said, "Let's see if you can ball like the way you did last night."

"Oh baby, it's on," he said, laughing as he positioned himself to return her volley.

They played three games of tennis—Tangi won the first game, Steele won the second, and Tangi won the third.

Sweat running down his face, his heart racing, Steele wanted to play another game.

With a round of rapid volley between them, Steele won another point to bring his score to 60. They were tied 2 to 2.

"One more game," Steele said between gulps of water.

Tangi thirstily drank from a bottle of water before moving back to her playing position. "It's a male ego thing, right?"

"It's a play-to-win thing."

Tangi walked toward the net to retrieve a tennis ball. "I'm going to beat you," she said, turning and walking to the court line, seductively sashaying her hips.

It was an intense round with long bouts of volleying in between bouts of playful bantering. Tangi swung hard, and Steele missed the volley.

"Game over," she gushed breathlessly. "I told you I was going to win."

"You had an unfair advantage."

She gave him an innocent look.

"Every time you walked that walk all I could think about was last night."

The innocent look turned smug. "I know."

"I want to paint you," Steele said, sitting across from Tangi at an outdoor café. "More water, please," he said when the waiter arrived with their meals. Still thirsty from the physical exertion of playing tennis, they drank down a second glass of icy cold water.

"Paint me?" Tangi said, holding the glass of water in her hand. "Is that something . . . sexual?"

"I want to do a portrait of you. I haven't painted in years, but for some reason I want to paint you."

"Not naked." She assumed by the tone of his voice that he was serious. She couldn't see his eyes hidden behind his dark shades. "I don't let anyone take pictures of me naked."

"I don't do nudes," he said. Reaching across the table, he touched her face. "You're beautiful. Hopefully I can capture all of your beauty. Can I paint you?"

Tangi pondered his request, trying to reign in the sensations in her heart. They were unfamiliar sensations for which she had no definition. "I'm flattered," she finally half-whispered.

"I haven't painted in years so you might not be flattered."

Gaining control of her emotions, she knew now was not the time to decipher the ramblings of her heart. "I have a feeling you're good at whatever you're passionate about." She drank more water. "When?"

"After we eat and get back to the hotel. I went

shopping for supplies this morning. Very limited selection, but I have what I need: brushes, paints, and a canvas."

"You're serious about this," Tangi said.

"I even found a spot where I can paint you. It's in the garden area, near the gazebo."

"You were busy shopping this morning and I was sleeping." She paused, before saying, "I went to sleep with you on my mind and woke up thinking about you."

He kissed the back of her hand. "You were on my mind the whole time."

Steele began with her face, choosing a mixture of brown, bronze, and copper to capture her skin tone. With each brush stroke, he felt that he was doing more than painting her. He hadn't painted in a long time, but an unknown power seemed to take over, guiding his brush strokes. With each sweep of the brush, he felt that he was connecting with his subject in an almost surreal way. He was so engrossed in her face, her beauty, the painting, that he didn't think about what was happening. If he stopped to think about it, he would have realized that each brush stroke was a stroke of love.

Tangi was also affected, but in a different kind of way. Posed in a supine position, with the lush gardens and colored foliage for scenery, she forgot that she was being painted. Her thoughts were on the man painting her. He was a fantasy, but he was also very real: somehow he'd connected with something inside her soul. She tried to ignore it, but lying there motionless, she had to face it. Her heart was coming alive for this man. *If this fantasy doesn't end soon, I could fall in love with him.*

Steele realized an outside force had possessed him when he viewed the finished painting. It was a work of art and way beyond his skill level. He'd never painted before with such talent, detail, and artistry. It truly resembled her, resonating the beauty of her spirit. He stared at his work—in total awe. It suddenly struck him that he was in awe of her—in awe of everything he knew about her and even the things he didn't know.

"I'm done," he finally said.

Tangi rose from the bench and walked slowly toward the canvas, uncertain of what she'd see, unsure that she'd like it. She hesitated briefly before turning to view the painting. "It's wonderful." she gushed in amazement. "You said you hadn't painted in years, but this is unbelievable! You're really good. It's beautiful."

With those words he knew what'd happened while painting her. "That's because you're beautiful," he said, kissing her gently on the mouth. It was a tender, soul-stirring kiss.

Suddenly, and unexpectedly, her cell phone rang. Tangi startled at the sound.

"That's your phone."

"Hello," she said, after digging through her purse to find the phone.

"I'm having a fabulous time," she said, when Adele asked if she was enjoying her vacation. "I'm having the best time of my life."

"Now it's time to come back to reality," Adele said.

The expression on Tangi's face changed when Adele told her about an audition to host a fashion-style show on VH5. Her face glistened with excitement. She knew her agent had lobbied hard to get her this audition, telling her that she'd only had a 30 percent chance of getting the audition.

"I'll be there," she said, disconnecting the call.

"Adele's the best—"

"The best what?"

She studied his face, then said, "If I tell you . . . the fantasy ends."

"So reality beckons."

Tangi didn't answer. She didn't need to. From the expression on her face, he knew their time together was coming to an end.

"I agree with you," Steele said. "I'm having the best time of my life."

"Let's not think about reality," Tangi said, gazing into his eyes. "Let's enjoy our time together."

"There's only one thing I want to do."

Back in his room, Steele drew her face up close to his, gazed into her eyes, then caressed her lips with his. This kiss was different. His tongue possessed her mouth, but in a different way. This kiss was more personal and intimate—and more revealing. It was sexually charged—not with lust and desire, but with unidentified emotions.

Every touch, kiss, and movement was laced with an undercurrent of emotion. When he entered her, they felt the splendor of the moment. Their hands clasped together, he moved slowly inside her, kissing her lips, the hollow of her shoulders, her ripe breasts. His movements were slow and deliberate, as if he wanted the moment to last forever.

Tangi didn't want him to stop. Each time he moved inside her she felt herself swirling deeper into the fantasy, but inside, it was mixing up with reality.

They moved together slowly. Hot sensations pulsed through their bodies.

Entwined together, Steele stopped, and stared into Tangi's eyes with such intensity of emotion that they shared the same thought: neither wanted the fantasy to end.

Overwhelmed with emotion, Steele stroked deeper and deeper, faster and faster—until they were both suspended in a moment of time.

Deep into the night, Steele drew her close to his body, and held her tight. "What if I want to contact you?"

"I don't know if we should. Part of me wants to but—"

"I want to know who you are," Steele said, his voice powered by heartfelt emotion, "where you come from, what you do."

"This was so perfect and so right. But if we take it outside of this time and place, it might not be so perfect."

Steele pondered that thought before saying, "Let's dare to find out."

"What if we're wrong? What if our lives don't connect? It'll ruin this memory."

"The only thing that'll ruin this is it ending."

Tangi was quiet for a long time. This was the most wonderful experience of her life, but it had to end. She had to face the truth and be strong; she had to let it go. "I don't think we should try to mix fantasy and reality."

"It frightens you?"

"More than you know," she said, struggling to keep tears from welling up in her eyes.

"I'll respect your wishes. But I think we should exchange numbers or e-mails, just in case . . ."

He didn't finish his sentence but both understood.

In case I change my mind. In case I decide I want to see you again, thought Tangi.

In case I have to reach you. In case I have to know you're all right, thought Steele. "I understand. That's how you want it to be. But if you change your mind, here's how you can reach me."

"Don't tell me your phone number. I'll hear your voice and I'll think about that sexy mouth of yours."

Steele got out of bed in search of a writing pad. Upon finding one, he wrote down his e-mail address and telephone numbers.

"My e-mail is *TE1111@aol.com.*"

Steele wrote down her e-mail address, but he knew he wouldn't forget it. Her address would be permanently etched in his mind.

"Put your number in the side pocket of my purse," Tangi said.

Steele slipped back under the covers, and drew her body close to his.

"Thank you for the best time of my life," Tangi said.

Kissing her gently on the neck, Steele whispered in her ear. "It's not over yet." He drew the covers back to behold the splendor of her beautiful body. "There will be no sleeping tonight."

Eight

"What's happening with the money?"

A Macanudo cigar in his hand, Rick Boullain leaned back in his sumptuous office chair and kicked a pair of gleaming Gucci's up onto his desk. "It's not a big deal, Devon." Unconcerned eyes stared into concerned ones. "You're panicking unnecessarily."

Devon stood in front of his partner's desk, hands on hips, incredulity in his eyes. "The payroll checks have bounced two times within the last three months, and I'm panicking?"

"It's not unusual for small companies like ours to have financial problems from time to time." He released a cloud of smoke. "Now, if we brought some investors into the company, our financial picture would be different."

"Wait a minute" Devon said, holding up both hands as if he were a cop stopping traffic. "You're not going to sideswipe me. We're not talking about investors. We're talking about the way you're handling company money."

Devon dropped into the leather chair facing Rick's desk. He studied his partner—a black-haired Caucasian man with clear blue eyes that seemed to have a hypnotic affect on women. Rick wasn't particularly handsome, but he was tall and well-built and the fact that he was the son of wealthy entrepreneur Richard Boullain, Sr. magnified his appeal to women.

Boullain Enterprises had investments in the oil and shipping industries, and in recent years, had expanded its financial interests into New Orleans' booming gambling industry. Considering the rumor that the family's wealth in the 1920s and 1930s originated from bootlegging whiskey and moonshine, their expansion into the gambling industry surprised very few in town. The Boullains were known for their business ventures as well as their personal escapades. They had a reputation for making generous donations to local charities, hospitals, and orphanages, but the Boullain family also had a scandalous reputation involving prostitutes, extra-marital affairs, and questionable campaign donations to certain political figures.

"Be straight with me, Rick. I want to know exactly what's going on." A reproving glare on his face, he wondered if Rick was going to be honest. "What's the real deal?"

As business partners, they were as different as night and day. There were the obvious differences: Devon was black and had a middle-class background; Rick was white and had a wealthy background. Then there were the not so obvious differences—personality and business style. Rick had a gregarious personality and liked being in the forefront, whereas Devon was quiet and laid-back and preferred to be in the background.

However, their business—WebGrooves—garnered

attention from the local business community. Rick pursed clients and handled financial and administrative manners, and Devon concentrated on the technical know-how and creative design skills required to build customized web sites. Their differences in strengths, in effect, offset the other's weaknesses.

Even though they were dissimilar in many ways, one similarity in particular was the glue that kept their partnership together: both had something to prove. Rick wanted to prove to his father that he could build a business from scratch and guide it to success. Devon wanted to prove to himself and his family, especially big brother Romare, that he could be successful.

An odd partnership—with foibles and foils—but one that for all intents and purposes had been working well—until now.

"Clients don't always pay on time like they're supposed to," Rick said, before inhaling his cigar.

"I thought we had an understanding that we—"

Rick's telephone rang. He checked the number in the caller ID box. "I need to take this call."

Devon observed the color drain from Rick's face when he answered the phone. Rick turned his chair in the opposite direction, but Devon could still hear the tension in his partner's voice. "I'll take care of it." His voice grew even more agitated. "I'll take care of it!"

While waiting for Rick to finish his call, he looked around the room. Rick's office felt more like a den than an office. The walls were decorated with pennants from New Orleans' professional football and basketball teams: the New Orleans

Saints and the Hornets, along with other sports memorabilia—a signed football helmet, a signed baseball, and framed autographed snapshots of Rick with professional athletes.

When Rick turned his chair back around, Devon knew something was wrong. "You look like you just heard from a ghost."

"I'm going to be a ghost," Rick mumbled.

Devon gaped at him. "What?"

"Ignore what I said." Rick looked away guiltily. "Just rambling about nothing."

"You should see your face, man! You don't look like it's nothing and it doesn't sound like it's nothing."

His head snapped around. "It's not your problem." Agitation and fear rang in his voice.

"So it has nothing to do with the business?"

Rick impatiently inclined his head. "No. Not at all." He went over to the bar and poured a healthy dose of Jack Daniel's into a glass.

"So it's not about the business, but whatever it is, it's got you scared," Devon said, observing Rick's twitching hands. "Why are you drinking in the middle of the day?"

"It's not a crime." Rick swallowed some whiskey; his face grimaced as the hundred-proof liquor surged down his throat. "My folks drink during the day. All the time, especially my dear mother."

"Look, Rick, I'm not trying to get into your personal life, but if there's anything I can do to help . . . let me know."

A twinge of guilt nudged Rick's conscience. He was lying to Devon, but he didn't know what else to do at the moment. Rick planted a crooked smile on his face. "Don't worry. It's my problem. I'll handle it."

Devon gave one last puzzled shake of his head before returning to the reason for their conversation. "Are you saying that our clients aren't paying on time?"

"They're supposed to pay within sixty days."

"Did Chandler and Chandler pay?"

Rick looked away, then picked up his glass of whiskey. "No."

"Stage 3 Chemicals?"

Rick swallowed some whiskey before saying, "No."

"And what about Advantage Technologies?"

"Yeah, yeah, they paid," Rick said, shrugging nonchalantly, but not revealing that the check was funneled into his private checking account. He consulted his watch, and then his cell phone rang. "I really have to go." He viewed his cell phone. "It's Isadora. I'm meeting her for lunch."

Devon's brows wrinkled together over a curious stare. "Who's that?"

"A woman I like to screw." He laughed. "She wants to get married. That's never going to happen."

"Rick, man, we have to get our finances together." Devon rose from his chair. "You need to make that your priority."

Porta Plataea was boring. Absolutely boring. The last three days of Steele's vacation were uneventful. The sun didn't glow, the sand didn't glisten, and the stars didn't sparkle.

Did the sun, sand, and stars change, or had he changed?

Steele grappled with that question for three long days. As much as he wanted to, he couldn't convince himself to believe something that was the byproduct of his delusional thoughts. The sun, sand, and stars hadn't changed. He'd changed.

He realized that Jane's presence was what turned the island into an extraordinary paradise. Without her, it was just paradise. The island's beauty was unchanged, yet it didn't feel the same. Jane had brought magic to it, but now she was gone. The effect of her presence festered inside his heart, soul, and mind, plaguing him with questions that were like an illness. Answers to the questions were the only remedy.

Who was she really?

Where did she go?

Would he ever see her again?

The questions haunted him so much that he inquired about Jane at the front desk.

"Sorry, sir. We are not at liberty to reveal our guests' identities," the front desk clerk explained. "It's their decision whether to disclose that information."

"Thank you for you help." With a polite smile, he requested to speak to the hotel manager. The hotel clerk escorted him to the nearby manager's office.

Inside the office, Steele sat down. The olive-skinned man on the opposite side of the desk had a foreign-look about him and spoke English with a hint of an accent. "How can I help you, sir?"

"I know you have a policy of anonymity, but I really need to find out the identity of woman who left two days ago." Drawing a deep breath, he continued. "She's honey-brown, drop dead gorgeous, and has a killer, sexy walk."

Tilting his head, the hotel manager gave him a thoughtful appraisal. "Sir, we don't—"

Ignoring the interruption, Steele went on. "She calls herself Jane. I don't know if that was her official alias with the hotel, but I would like to know her real name. I'm hoping you'll make an exception to your policy."

"I apologize, sir. But it's absolutely forbidden. No exceptions are allowed."

The walls of his heart felt as thin as those of a balloon about to burst. Even though he knew there was only a remote possibility that the hotel manager would make an exception, Steele was nonetheless disappointed. Somehow the words "I understand" came out of his mouth, confusing his heart with their betrayal.

"It happens all the time. People come here, meet someone and have a fantastic time, and then it's over." A sympathetic smile was on the hotel manager's face. "Sooner or later, everybody has to go back to their real lives."

Steele rose from his chair. Embarrassed that he'd acted like a teenager mourning the loss of a high school crush, he mumbled, "Thank you," and quickly left the hotel manager's office.

His flight back to New Orleans was the next day. He was glad to be leaving boring Porta Plataea.

"You're not in Porta Plataea?" Gillian asked Tangi over the phone.

"I'm in good old New York, where I just auditioned to be the host of a brand new fashion show on VH5! It's going to be called *Places and People of Style* or *People and Places of Style*. Excuse me for screaming in your ear. Yes, yes, yes!"

Gillian laughed. "So, you're excited about it."

"I hope I get! I hope I get it!"

"What does Adele think?"

"They're still defining the show, so they're not sure whether they want a model or "real journalist" type. I don't know which way it's going to go."

"How did the audition go?" Lounging in her bed, Gillian leaned back against the pillows. The eleven o'clock news was on the television.

"It went great! I was kind of surprised at myself. I thought I was going to freeze-up, but I didn't. I had to do a take reading lines from a teleprompter, and then I did an interview."

"It sounds like a wonderful opportunity."

"And Romare is going to say: 'she's finally using her education.'"

"Speaking of my wonderful husband," Gillian said, tapping Romare's arm, "he wants to speak to you."

"Okay, but I want to say hi to Jordy and Nolan."

"They're asleep, girl. Do you know what time it is?"

Tangi checked her bedside clock. "My body doesn't know what time zone I'm in. Girl, I met someone." Her voice filled with excitement. "I'll tell you all about him after I talk to Romare."

"She met somebody," Gillian whispered, while handing Romare the phone.

"Tangi, are you okay?" Romare asked.

"I'm fine, big brother. Why are you tripping?"

"Just a little worried. I thought you might have been depressed about Brock and gone into exile."

"I told you I was sad about him for about ten seconds. I really needed to get some R & R. My body was just worn out."

"I just wanted to make sure nothing else was going on."

"I'm cool."

"When are you coming to see us?" Romare asked.

"Probably in a week or so."

"Okay. Love you. Here's Gillian."

Gillian put the receiver to her ear. "Hey, girl, who did you meet?"

"John Doe."

"Tangi, surely you didn't let some man convince you that his name is John Doe."

"No. I'm not crazy. I didn't want to tell him who I was and somehow we decided not to reveal our real identities. He called me Jane and I called him John."

"Oh."

"He's the most wonderful, genuine person I've met in a long time," Tangi gushed. "We had a fabulous time. If this audition hadn't come up I'd still be there with him."

"I haven't heard you sound this excited about someone . . . ever."

"We just connected with each other. There was this vibe between us." The memory of his touch made her pause. "We didn't have to filter through I'm-a-celebrity and all that craziness."

"I'm confused. Was he a celebrity, too? How come you didn't recognize each other?"

"He's not a celebrity. He wanted to tell me who he was. I was the one who kept insisting that we keep our identities a secret," Tangi explained. "I don't know why, but he didn't recognize me. I think that's why we had such a good time."

"So now what?"

"I don't know. I told him that it was an island fling and that we should leave it there, but I can't stop thinking about him."

"Can you contact him?"

"Yes, but I haven't." She exhaled a deep breath. "I'm kind of waiting to see if that feeling is going to stay with me. If it does, then maybe it was more than an island fling."

"Just listening to your voice, it sounds like it was."

"So anyway, what's been going on since I've been gone?"

"My mother's in the hospital. She had a heart attack."

"Oh no, why didn't you tell me?"

"I didn't want to intrude on your interlude."

"Gillian, you should have called. I know how close Mama Ruby is to Jordy and Nolan. She's dear to my heart." Her voice relayed concern and compassion. "Is she going to be released soon?"

Gillian didn't immediately answer. "She's going have a major operation. A triple bypass."

"Oh, I'm so sorry to hear that. How's Jordy handling it?"

"Trying to be tough. She hasn't seen her yet. If all goes well, they're going to move her from ICU to a regular room for a couple of days before the surgery." Gillian felt a nervous flutter in her stomach, the thought of her mother's surgery and the possible outcome was unsettling. "We're hoping they move her tomorrow and then we'll take Jordy to see her."

Tangi was quiet for a moment. "Gillian, I'll be there tomorrow."

"You don't have to," she protested. "I know you're busy."

"I'm just waiting to hear if I'm going to get a call back, and that could be next week or next month. I know it won't be in the next couple of days, so I can come see you guys."

"If you insist," she said, then whispered to Romare, "Tangi's coming tomorrow." Speaking into the phone, she said, "We'll come pick you up."

"You don't have to do that."

"I know how you much like it when we meet you at the airport."

"Yeah, I do," she said in a tender tone. "I'll have Adele call with the flight information. You know it's going to be a late flight."

"I know. Nolan loves going to the airport to get Auntie T. See you tomorrow," Gillian said before hanging up.

Nine

The 747's wheels hit the runway at a high speed, steadily decreasing until the plane came to a stop at its terminal destination at Louis Armstrong New Orleans International Airport. Steele checked his watch: it was 11:00 P.M. He released a long sigh of relief. Not because the plane ride had been turbulent or choppy. It had been a long flight, but smooth and problem-free. He sought refuge from memories of Jane in a book, but the words couldn't obscure her eerie presence. The book would have held his attention if it were about Jane, it contained her picture, or it revealed her identity.

Steele was relieved to be back home—thousands of miles away from Porta Plataea, the island where he tumbled from the heights of happiness to the depths of loneliness—a long drop in a very short period of time. He was back in familiar territory, and he wouldn't feel so out-of-place. Work would engulf him as usual. He'd have cases to prosecute and he still had to prepare for his lecture series. Steele hoped that once he returned to his normal routine, memories of Jane would dissipate.

But he knew it was a band-aid approach to something that required a different kind of healing, a healing that only Jane could provide. He needed to talk to her, hear her voice, see her smile. He'd decided to wait until he returned home to contact her. The urge to get in touch with her was very powerful. It took every ounce of self-control not to yield to the temptation. In part, it was self-defense. He didn't want her to think that she'd become the CEO of his thoughts. But she had.

He definitely didn't want her to think that she'd successfully infiltrated the force field guarding his heart. He hadn't quite come to that conclusion.

And it was her game they were playing. The next move was hers.

Steele didn't depart from the plane until the flight attendant brought him the painting of Jane. He'd requested special storage on the plane to prevent damage to his most treasured vacation mementos. The sudden thought that he'd never see her again chilled his very soul. He shook his head as if to whisk away the possibility.

"Thank you," he said to the flight attendant, and then moved down the ramp into the terminal.

Steele strode through the airport's terminal mindlessly following the signs to baggage claim. Yawning, his mind on plans for the next day, he grabbed his suitcases from the baggage carousel. A familiar walk caught his peripheral vision—sashaying hips, swishing buttocks—Jane's sexy walk. His heart rate accelerated. He dropped his suitcases and turned in the woman's direction, but several people surrounded her. He couldn't see her face, only her back, and from a distance, she appeared to be Jane's height. She was holding a little boy whose arms were tightly wrapped around her.

Could it be her?

He stepped closer, his view now blocked by a tall black man. She claimed she wasn't married, but did she lie? Maybe she was escaping from her family. Was the man her husband? Who was the woman? The young girl looked too old to be her daughter, unless she had had her when she was very, very young.

But it didn't make sense. It didn't match up to her veiled description of her life. Did she leave out some important pieces? Was that why she insisted on complete anonymity? None of his speculations measured up to his perceptions about her. Maybe they were misconceptions based on a case of deception.

Steele knew it would be rude to interrupt the happy family gathering, and he would be very embarrassed if he were wrong. And it was very late. Yet, he was willing to risk humiliation to find out if this woman was indeed Jane.

A pair of wide, pouty lips stopped Steele.

They belonged to Nicole Kirkland.

"I missed you, lover," she said, wrapping her arms around his neck and covering his lips with hers.

"Nicole, what are you doing here?"

She narrowed her wide eyes. "That's a warm and fuzzy greeting." She removed her arms from around his neck. "I guess I won't ask if you missed me."

Steele ignored the remark. He didn't want to hurt her feelings. "I don't remember asking you to meet me at the airport."

"You didn't." She placed her hands on her healthy hips as if to showcase her hourglass figure in the form-fitting, sleeveless dress she was wearing. "I wanted to surprise you."

"You definitely surprised me," Steele said, angling his head to view the woman he thought was Jane. But, she wasn't there. He looked toward the automatic exit doors, but she wasn't there either. He saw some people getting into a Lincoln Navigator, but he didn't see Jane.

"Who are you looking for?" Nicole asked.

He turned back around and faced his on-again, off-again lover. "Someone I met on the plane." He picked up his suitcases and forced a smile on his face. "Thanks for coming to get me, especially since it's so late."

"You're welcome." Nicole didn't hide her disappointment that Steele was unenthusiastic about her presence. "I know you want to get home," she said coolly.

"I'm absolutely exhausted."

"I wasn't planning on staying," she said.

"Thanks for being so understanding," he said, genuinely relieved that he didn't have to feign interest in a sexual liaison. He wasn't in the mood and he didn't feel the desire he usually felt for her.

"I've been there. I know what an island fling can do to you." Nicole gave him an all-knowing smile. She wanted him to know that she knew that he'd spent time with another woman. Her plans to take their sex-only relationship to the next level would have to wait. Steele was difficult to emotionally penetrate, and she thought she'd managed to crack his exterior wall. But whomever he met had somehow managed to get further penetration than she had. She would have to give him time to recover.

Steele simply smiled, a benign smile, neither confirming nor denying her statement. They both knew that she was right.

"Auntie Tangi, Auntie Tangi, did you see fish in the water?"

"All kinds of fish—red fish, blue fish—"

"Yellow fish, green fish," he said. "That's like my book. It's Daddy's favorite book, too."

"The fish I saw were prettier than any fish in a Dr. Seuss book," Tangi said.

"I'm sleepy Auntie Tangi, Auntie Tangi." Nolan yawned.

"I know it. It's way past your bedtime. You can go to sleep."

"Will you be here when I wake up?"

"Yes, baby boy."

"Now go to sleep so I can talk to Auntie Tangi," Jordy said, squeezing closer to Tangi, who sat between them.

"So much love. I can feel it." Tangi leaned forward and tapped Gillian's shoulder. "You want to sit beside me, too?"

Gillian laughed.

"You're so silly, Auntie Tangi. I have something very important to tell you. It's my big surprise." Jordy creased her brows. "Auntie Gigi, did you tell her?"

"No. I promised you I wouldn't tell her."

"Uncle Romare, did you tell her?" Jordy asked.

"I wouldn't dare spill the beans."

"Tell me, tell me!" Tangi laughed. "I'm started to sound like Nolan, repeating myself."

"I'm going to be famous like you."

"You are?"

"You're Tyra Banks famous and I'm going to be Halle Berry famous."

"You're going to be in a movie?"

"I'm going to be in a play at school. I got the lead part in *The Wizard of Oz.*"

"You go, girl." Tangi kissed Jordy's forehead. "Somewhere over the rainbow," she said, singing the famous song.

"It's a hard song to sing. My drama teacher says I should get a voice coach," Jordy explained.

"How does Sterling feel about her interest in acting?" Tangi asked, referring to Jordy's biological father, the first black judge appointed to the Louisiana's state court. Jordy didn't know he was her father until her mother was murdered while writing an expose on the oil industry. Gillian's investigation into her sister's death yielded unexpected fruit—Jordy's father.

"Surprisingly," Gillian said, "he's okay with it."

"He thinks it's just a phase and that I'll come to my senses and want to be an lawyer like him," added Jordy.

"Time will tell," Romare said.

A yawn burst from Jordy's mouth. "I'm sleepy, too," she said, leaning her head against Tangi's shoulder. "I have some other good news. I'm going to see grandma tomorrow."

"So, they moved her out of ICU." Tangi yawned. "That is good news."

Within the next moments, the only sound Romare heard was the cacophony of snores in the back seat and in the seat beside him.

Ten

"Where did you get that beautiful painting?"

Steele spun away from his computer and saw his sister Jana Grayson Keyes staring at the painting of Jane he'd hung over the sofa in the den opposite his desk. He stared at the picture and felt himself swirling in the memories: the mysterious force that overcame him while painting her and the mysticism of their erotic night of passion that went beyond his imagination.

"Steele," she said, nudging his shoulder.

"I got it in Porta Plataea." He sipped from a tall glass of iced tea. "I painted it."

Jana glanced from the painting to Steele and back to the painting, disbelief on her face. "Stop playing!"

"I'm not."

Something in the tone of his voice made Jana repeat her actions. This time when she looked at her brother, surprise etched her dainty features. "You painted it? I can't believe it!" She moved in for a closer inspection. "This is a work of art."

"*She* is a work of art." His voice was full of undisguised lust and admiration.

"Whoa! I have to sit down for this." She flounced

over to the leather sofa and plopped down. "I have never heard you say anything like that before. It's the way you said it that's so profoundly different." She leveled her gaze in his direction. "Tell me, who the hell is she?"

"You're not going to believe me." Steele chuckled. "It's a profoundly different story."

Jana tilted her head to view the picture. "She looks familiar. She's somebody famous."

"I don't know who she is."

"What?" A deep crease furrowed her brow.

"I don't know who she is."

"Please explain." An impish grin on her face, she added, "About the night in question or about the nights in question."

"I know this sounds crazy, but I met this woman. We flirted with each other, and when I asked her who she was, she didn't want to say. We started playing this alias name game, if you will. I called her Jane and she called me John."

"How original," drolled Jana.

"We had a fantastic time. She's smart, beautiful, fun, and sexy."

"Oooh, a sexy girl," Jana teased.

"The more time we spent together, the more I wanted to know who she was. But she insisted that part of the fun was the mystery of not knowing who we really were."

"That's kind of deep." Jana pressed her back against the sofa. "How did you end up painting her?"

"One night we talked about childhood dreams. I mentioned that, at one time, I wanted to be a painter when I grew up. I told her I still dabbled with it, and that I paint every now and then," Steele explained. "The next day I decided I wanted to paint her, so I went out and bought a canvas and some paints and brushes."

Steele paused to stare at the painting. He was quiet for a moment, and then said, "When I painted her, something came over me. I've never painted anything like that in my life." His eyes connected with his sister's probing gaze. "It was the most surreal experience."

"You're a natural artist, Steele." Amusement lit Jana's face. "You have a gift; you just didn't pursue it. If I remember correctly you didn't want to be a *starving* artist."

He shrugged his shoulders. "Precisely."

"So what happened? How did it end?"

"She had to leave unexpectedly." Steele grew quiet, reflecting on their last night together of seemingly unquenchable passion.

"And—"

"I gave her my cell and home number and e-mail address. She gave me her e-mail address. I was just checking to see if she'd e-mailed me." Disappointment claimed his face. "She hasn't."

"That definitely is a profoundly different story."

Steele laughed. "Sound crazy?"

"Sounds like a fantasy." She caught a glimpse of longing in her brother's face. "But you want the fantasy to continue." It was more a statement than a question.

He stared at the picture a moment before meeting his sister's probing gaze. "It's that obvious?"

"It's written all over your face, big brother." Jana

studied her brother's work of art. "She's somebody famous."

"I considered that possibility, but then I dismissed it. She doesn't act like a prima donna. She's warm and friendly and . . . normal."

"So maybe she's not your typical celebrity."

He shrugged his shoulder. "You know how I feel about celebrities."

"All celebrities aren't like your father."

"Ouch." He rubbed his cheek as if her comment stung his face.

"You haven't called her?" Jana asked.

He shook his head.

"So you're playing the waiting game. You're waiting for her to make the first move.

Steele laughed. "It's her game and it's her turn."

"If I were a betting woman, I'd say you're going to make the first move."

"If I were a betting man, I wouldn't bet against you."

They both laughed.

"Grandma!"

Ruby's eyes sprung open when she heard Jordy's voice. Her heart began to race as indicated by the beeping sounds on the hospital monitoring equipment growing louder. Nurse Camille McDeal Grayson, standing next to the bed, eyed the numbers on the equipment monitoring her patient's vital signs. A hint of concern gleamed in the nurse's eyes as she watched the numbers dramatically rise. But when Camille observed the bright smile on Ruby's face, her concern melted away. The higher pulse and heartbeat numbers weren't due to Ruby's heart condition, but from excitement over seeing her family.

"Child, come give your grandmother a big ol' hug."

Remembering Gillian's warnings, Jordy carefully hugged her grandmother, mindful of the I.V. needles attached to her arms. "I'm so glad you're doing better."

"Me, too, darling. Me, too. I can't wait to get out of this place. That ICU is really the pits." Ruby crunched her face into a scowl. "I don't like the nurses," she complained. "Except Ms. Camille. She been real nice to me."

"Hello, pretty girl," Camille said, smiling at Jordy.

"Hello," Jordy said.

"Your grandmother is a sweet lady. I love taking care of her." Camille looked at Ruby. "I need to check on something. I'll be back shortly," she said, before leaving the room.

"I was scared, Grandma," Jordy said, settling into the bedside chair.

"Me, too. But your grandma is a fighter. She ain't ready to leave this here place."

"You can't." Jordy's face was full of emotion. "You have to see me in my school play. I'm going to be Dorothy in *The Wizard of Oz*."

"I'm so proud of you." Ruby stared at her granddaughter's pre-pubescent face—large brown eyes, bright smile, and chubby cheeks on a round face. She was getting prettier every day and looking more and more like her mother. "You know your mama is proud of you, too. She's smiling down from heaven at you."

Jordy didn't know what to say. People often said those very words to her. Hearing those words made her feel happy, but sometimes it made her feel sad. It made her feel happy today.

"We have to rehearse a lot," Jordy said, "but I don't mind."

"You keeping up with your school work?"

"Yes, ma'am," Jordy said, recalling Gillian's warning that if her grades slipped, she couldn't be in the play.

"That's a good girl."

Jordy heard a light tapping on the door. A knowing look on her face, she squeezed her grandmother's hands. "Grandma, you have a surprise visitor."

"Who could that be? I ain't exactly dressed for company." Ruby surveyed the room for her personal belongings. "I don't know where my wig is."

"Mama Ruby you don't have to dress up for me."

"Tangi, is that you?" Ruby asked, even though she'd recognized the voice. She just couldn't believe that her son-in-law's sister was visiting her.

"Yes, ma'am."

"Well, I'll be! You took time out of your busy schedule to see me."

"I had to, Mama Ruby. I had to come and make sure these doctors are treating you right." Tangi strutted into the room smelling of jasmine and musk. She kissed Ruby on the cheek. "I heard you couldn't have flowers in ICU, but get ready because you're about to have a garden in here."

Ruby's eyes widened with anticipation. "A garden?"

"Yes ma'am. I know how you love flowers," Tangi

said, "so within the next hour, there's going to be flowers everywhere."

"Everywhere." Jordy spread her arms wide. "You're going to love it!"

"You done gave me something to look forward to, besides seeing my grandbabies."

Nurse Grayson returned to Ruby's room, immediately noticing the accelerated numbers on the monitoring equipment. "Now who is this that's got your heart rate up?"

Ruby, Tangi, and Jordy looked at the monitors for a moment before returning their gaze on the nurse. They didn't know what the flashing numbers meant.

"Is my grandmother going to be all right?" Fear radiated from Jordy's face.

"Oh sugar pie, your grandmother's fine. These machines pick up every little thing," Camille said, flashing a reassuring smile at Jordy. "It's nothing serious. She's just a little excited because of her visitors."

"Oh!" A look of relief replaced the look of worry on Jordy's face. "She's excited because of Auntie Tangi. She's a famous model."

"She is?" Camille's gaze went from Tangi to Jordy.

"Yes ma'am," Jordy said proudly.

"Hello, I'm Tangi Ellington," she said, smiling at Camille.

"She does runway shows for famous designers. She's been on the cover of forty-four magazines."

"Wow!" Camille tilted her head, a warm smile on her face. "What a pleasure and honor to meet you."

"Likewise," Tangi said.

"I'll come back later, Miss Ruby." Camille

squeezed her patient's hand. "When your visitors are gone."

"All right," Ruby said.

"Enjoy your visit," was the nurse's departing remark to Tangi and Jordy.

"Is Nolan coming?" Ruby asked, her eyes on Tangi.

"Gillian's going to bring him this afternoon for a short visit," Tangi said.

"I just want to hug him and tell him I love him." Ruby affectionately rubbed Jordy's cheek. "I love you too, Jordy. And don't you ever forget it."

Network bandwidth was on Devon's mind. Did Stage 3 Chemicals' network have the technical infrastructure to support the new web site he was designing? Initially, they did. But Devon woke up in the middle of the night worried that the web site—with the latest technology and design approach—would shut down the company's network.

The next morning he scheduled a meeting with the company's information technology department for that very same day. He'd even directed the members of his design team to cease working on Stage 3 Chemicals' web site until he had more technical details.

It was the details of Devon's face that Veronica Hamilton noticed as he sat in the lobby of Stage 3 Chemicals—his brown eyes, angular nose, broad mouth, and beard. And there was another all-important detail she observed: he wasn't wearing a wedding band.

Veronica had heard that the web designer was handsome, but she'd never seen him because she was usually stuck in her cubicle performing her accounting clerk responsibilities. Today was her lucky day: she finally got to see Devon Ellington and he was indeed a handsome young brother.

She was filling in for the receptionist when Devon walked in. She knew who he was even before he introduced himself and requested to see the director of information technology.

She flashed her biggest smile at Devon before calling the director and informing him of Devon's arrival. Veronica watched him sit on the sofa and stretch out his long legs. This wasn't the right time or the right place, but it would probably be the only opportunity she'd have to ask him out to dinner. Veronica wasn't going to let the opportunity pass her by, so she skipped the "how's the weather?" and "what's traffic like out there?" chatter.

"I heard the new web site is going to be the bomb!"

Devon laughed. "I can't imagine those words coming out of Robert's mouth."

"He's such a geek," Veronica said. "I figured they must really be happy with your work because we already sent you—I mean your company—a check. Usually we don't pay until the project is done. Most of the times it's thirty to sixty days after it's done. You guys must have really blown their socks off."

Devon narrowed his gaze at the woman behind the desk. The fact that she was pretty, petite, and dark-brown skinned with green eyes barely registered. "What did you say?" His eyes focused on the nametag on the desk. "Elizabeth."

"My name isn't Elizabeth. She's out sick today. I'm Veronica Hamilton."

"Hello, Veronica." Devon forced a smile on his face. "How do you know about the check?"

"I work in accounting."

"You're sure a check was sent to WebGrooves?"

"Positive." Knowing that any second he'd be whisked away to his meeting, Veronica surrendered to the impulse of instant attraction, "Devon, I think you're a very attractive and intelligent brother." She batted her green eyes and smiled. "Can we go out to dinner one night?"

It wasn't the first time a woman had asked him out. But, he was thinking about that check, so his response was delayed. "Sure," he said, feigning a look of interest. She was an attractive woman, but he had no desire to date anyone other than Brielle. They hadn't spoken of a formal commitment, but it was communicated non-verbally in many ways. He liked the direction of their relationship. "Why don't you give me your number?" he said, not wanting to offend Veronica.

Her eyes lit up. She quickly jotted her number down on a slip of paper and handed it to Devon. "One day soon."

Before Devon could respond, the IT director entered the lobby. "We're ready to meet with you, Devon."

"Great." Devon rose from the sofa. He flashed a smile at Veronica. She thought it was a flirtatious smile, but it was a deceptive smile. He hoped it hid his anger. At that moment, he wasn't thinking about taking her to dinner, nor was he thinking about Stage 3 Chemicals' web site. He was thinking about his conversation with Rick Boullain. He claimed that Stage 3 Chemicals hadn't paid them. But Rick had lied.

Had he lied about any other checks?

Eleven

"Tangi made dinner."

Devon's mouth watered in anticipation of eating his favorite food made his favorite way—food he'd eaten as a child, food that reeled him backward in time to memories of his mother cooking in the kitchen wearing an apron imprinted with the words MOM'S KITCHEN. STAY OUT OF MY POTS. "I'm going to stuff myself like a pig."

"Come in, Mr. Pig." Gillian hugged her brother-in-law. "And please introduce me to your friend."

"Gillian, this is Brielle Mitchell." He put an arm around Brielle's shoulders. "This is my sister-in-law Gillian Ellington."

Brielle extended her hand. "It's very nice to meet you."

"We don't shake hands, Brielle. We're a hugging family." Gillian embraced the thin, light-skinned young woman. "Welcome to my home."

"Thank you for inviting me."

"Devon's been talking about you a lot, so it's about time I met you." Gillian ushered them inside. "Come in and make yourselves at home. I have to run upstairs for a minute. Everybody's in the kitchen."

"She's so nice," Brielle said after Gillian was gone. "And your sister, a famous model, made dinner—"

"Tangi likes to cook." Devon shrugged his shoulders. "She always has."

"I can't believe I'm going to have dinner prepared by a supermodel," Brielle gushed with fanatic-like enthusiasm.

"Don't get all celebrity crazy. She gets enough of that when she's out in public."

"So I won't tell her I admire her and that I'm her number one fan and I think she's the—"

"You're so not funny," he said before planting a kiss on her cheek. Staring at her for a moment, he realized how proud he was to introduce her to his family. She was very attractive and quite intelligent. Cropped curly hair showcased her large brown eyes and luscious lips. And she was a techno-geek like him.

"You're smiling. You haven't smiled all evening."

His smile had disappeared with the memory of his conversation with the accounting clerk from Stage 3 Chemicals. Her innocent remark had an eerie portentousness. He couldn't concentrate on the meeting, occupied with derogatory thoughts about Rick Boullain. He tried to reach Rick, but he was again mysteriously missing-in-action. His disappearances were occurring more frequently. The fact that Rick wasn't returning his calls made him even angrier. It was obvious that WebGrooves was not his main focus. Even though Devon suspected that Rick was involved in something unsavory and, perhaps, dangerous, dipping into the company's funds was out of line.

"I'm sorry, baby." Brielle patted his cheek. "I wasn't trying to upset you."

"It's work stuff and I really don't want to think about it right now. I just want to enjoy an evening with my family."

Brielle nodded, and followed Devon into the kitchen.

"Hey, hey, everybody," Devon said.

"Uncle Devon, Uncle Devon" Nolan said, running toward him.

Devon picked up his nephew and kissed him on the cheek. "You're getting heavy."

"And tall," Nolan said. "Daddy says I'm growing like a weed."

"Brielle, this is my nephew, Nolan."

Brielle smiled at the little boy whose face was as round as a pie and his smile as wide as the moon. "He's so cute and adorable."

"I'm so cute and adorable," Nolan said.

Everyone laughed.

"Hey everybody, this is Brielle Mitchell," Devon said, when the laughter died down. "Brielle, that's my big brother Romare—"

"Hello, Brielle," Romare said.

"My niece Jordy."

"Hi," Jordy said with a friendly wave.

"And my little sister Tangi, who I hope made crab cakes and jambalaya."

"You know I did, D," Tangi said, while removing a pan from the oven. She came around the island and greeted Brielle with a hug. "I'm so glad to meet you."

"Me, too," Brielle gushed.

"You're shocked that I'm cooking?"

"Well . . . yes."

"I love to cook, but I have a confession. I hate to clean up."

"Auntie Gigi and I are the clean up crew," Jordy said.

"I help." Devon said.

"When? Tell me, when?" Gillian asked.

"On rare occasions," Devon admitted.

"Everything's ready," Tangi said, "so we can go into the dining room and eat."

"Yeah!" Nolan said. "I'll lead the way."

Everyone gathered around the dining room table. They held hands and closed their eyes while Romare offered a dinner prayer. The feast and conversation then began.

"Pass the bread."

"I'll just have water."

"Please pass the salt and pepper."

"This is delicious."

"Nothing like a home cooked meal."

"I want some more crab cakes."

"I want some rolls. They taste so good."

"So, how was your escape to paradise?" Devon asked Tangi.

"Heavenly. It felt so good to just relax. You were right, D. It was time for me to rest."

"Where did you go?" Brielle asked.

"To a beautiful resort in the Caribbean. Porta Plataea."

"She met somebody down there that she likes," Jordy said.

"Jordy," Gillian said in a scolding tone. "Were you on the phone listening to our conversation?"

"No."

"How did you know about it?"

"You were talking about it in the car."

Tangi laughed. "We thought you didn't know what we were talking about."

"I'm not dumb, you know," Jordy said.

"No one thinks that," Romare said.

"So, tell me about him," Devon said.

"She'll have to fill you in later when there are no ears around," Gillian said.

"I know you're talking about me." Jordy placed her hands over her ears. "You can talk. I just won't listen."

"How's Mama Ruby?" inquired Devon.

"She's making progress," Romare said.

"I went to see her two days ago," Jordy said. "She looked kind of tired, but she's going to be okay. Tangi went to see her, too."

"She's going to have surgery the day after to-morrow," Gillian said. "I'm keeping the faith that she's going to be all right."

"She is, Auntie Gigi. Grandma said she's not ready to leave."

The adults traded concerned looks, but re-frained from responding to Jordy's remark.

"How're things going with work?" Romare asked.

"I'll fill you in later when there are no ears around," Devon said.

"I'm not a baby you know," Jordy said.

"You did get those images I e-mailed you," Gillian asked Devon.

"Sure did," he answered.

"So tell us, how did you two meet?" Tangi asked.

Brielle blushed.

"Oh no," Jordy said, covering her ears.

"We met online."

Romare's eyebrows stretched. "A computer dating service?"

"Not through a dating site," Devon explained. "It was through a chat room."

"Like that sounds better," teased Tangi.

"There's a raging debate about new web technology. She posted her views and I didn't agree with them, so we had this ongoing debate."

"You never told me that part," Gillian said.

"I know. I didn't because of the way you'd react." Devon pointed to Romare and mocked the expression on his face.

"It sounds so geeky," Brielle said. "One day Devon said he wanted to see what I looked like. He said he was going to print my picture and then throw darts at it when we were debating."

"I was joking," Devon said.

"So I sent the picture. He immediately sent me an instant message. Instead of debating about web technology, we debated whether we should meet each other."

"This is interesting," said Tangi.

"I was pro, of course," said Devon.

"I was con, until he e-mailed his picture."

"After two weeks of e-mails and instant messages, we finally met each other." Devon stroked Brielle's cheek with his finger. "We looked at each other and just clicked."

"Like when you click the mouse button on the computer?" Nolan asked.

Tangi, Romare, Gillian, Devon, and Brielle laughed.

Jordy and Nolan exchanged baffled expressions.

"What did I say?" Nolan asked with the most innocent look on his face.

"Hey, Mama."

On bended knees, Camille looked up from the garden she was tending into her son's amused eyes. "It's about time you came around to see me."

"I've called several times, and you've always been at work," Steele said.

"I know," she said, extending him her hand.

He reached for her hand, supporting her weight as she awkwardly rose from her kneeling position, and kissed her on the cheek. "Are you sure you should be doing this when you're in pain?" he asked, even though it was a moot question. Gardening and reading were her favorite leisure-time activities.

"My arthritis was just acting up a little bit. I took some Motrin, so the pain should go away soon."

"Take a break," said Steele, escorting his mother up the three steps to the screened-in front porch of the three-bedroom, black shuttered ranch style house he grew up in.

Camille eased down onto the flower-painted glider, which matched the patio set that included a lounge, rocking chair, and table. "I sure could use something to drink."

Steele laughed at his mother's heavy hint. "I'm sure you have some tea. I'll bring you some."

He went inside the house, and five minutes later, returned with two glasses of syrupy sweet iced tea. He gave one to his mother and then sat down beside her. Stretching out his legs, he took long sips of the orange-flavored tea.

"You look relaxed," remarked Camille. "I think you really needed that vacation."

Steele nodded as memories of Jane invaded his mind. He couldn't think of Porta Plataea without thinking of Jane. It didn't take much, it seemed, to trigger memories of Jane. She was always there, lurking in his thoughts, teasing his heart. Every day he awakened with her on his mind. At night, he thought about her before going to sleep. Sleep was his only reprieve from her lingering presence.

Every morning, he'd tell himself not to think about her. It was a fling, a moment of lust, just for that moment in time. He tried to shut down thoughts of her, but he couldn't quite close the door on those memories.

"I had a good time."

"Meet anybody special?"

"You are so transparent," he teased, looking at his mother's mole-speckled caramel-colored face. An attractive woman in her early fifties, Camille was energetic and fun-loving. "I know Jana's already told you about her. She can't keep a secret for a minute."

"I want to hear about it from you."

"To be honest, Mama, I'm trying to forget about it. She has her life and I have mine." He shrugged with a casualness he didn't feel. "We had fun."

"You're having a hard time forgetting her, huh?" Amusement danced in her eyes, and empathy resounded in her voice.

"I must be transparent, too."

"Boy, I'm your mama. I know when your heart and spirit are unsettled."

"Jana told you everything?"

"We don't keep many secrets around here. I just found it interesting. It sounds like something from a romance novel. You spend time together, fall in love, and you don't even know each other's name."

Steele bristled. "I didn't say I fell in love with her."

Camille cocked an eyebrow, an impudent expression on her face. "You didn't say you didn't."

Steele let out a heavy breath. Was that why he couldn't forget about her? Had he fallen in love with her? A plot from one of his mother's romance novels certainly couldn't possibly apply to him. "The point is, the vacation is over and I'm back to reality."

"I'm dying to see that painting."

Steele shook his head. "Jana has such a big mouth."

"She says it's beautiful." She wagged her finger at him. "You should have studied art."

As a teenager, he'd entertained notions of becoming an artist. When he wasn't drawing or painting, he would visit galleries or museums. He went to college with the intention of becoming an artist, but in his junior year, he decided to major in pre-law.

"I didn't want to be the starving artist. But I will admit that painting her reminded me of how much I really enjoy it. I started a new painting the other day."

"She left a mark on you."

He gave his mother a quizzical look. "I don't like the way that sounds."

"It's just an old saying." Changing the conversation, she said, "I met a famous model the other day. She came to visit one of my patients."

"Really."

"I didn't know who she was, but some of the other nurses were going on about her. I can't remember her name." Trying to remember, she creased her brows together. "I think it began with a T."

"Tyra Banks? She's probably the only model I know."

"It wasn't her." Camille shook her head. "Anyway, she was very nice and down to earth. I didn't know who she was. I don't pay attention to these new singers and actors. I know the folks from my day." She drank the rest of her tea. "Something's troubling you about the job. It's been troubling you for a while."

A thoughtful look descended upon Steele's face as he stared into the distance. He didn't see the single-level houses in his line of vision across the street. He was reflecting on the crossroads in his life, in particular a crossroad he had reached just before taking his vacation. The sense of urgency in choosing his path had been magnified since returning from vacation. The Porta Plataea experience had changed him and whetted his appetite for change.

"It never made any sense to me how you could leave a beautiful law office and go work for the government."

"Sometimes I didn't feel like a lawyer."

"I don't know what that means."

"It paid very well, but it wasn't exciting. I went into law because I wanted to be a part of the justice system. I wanted to help victims of crime."

"Because of what happened to Matthew's mother," Camille said, referring to his best friend from high school whose mother was mysteriously killed. The News Orleans Police Department didn't seriously investigate the case, so the murderer was never found. For Matthew, it became an open wound that festered, turning him from an A student into an F student; he dropped out of high school. After a wild, self-destructive period, Matthew finished high school, college, and even law school.

"On some levels that influenced my decision to become a lawyer. I became a DA to help victims of crime. But the reality is that you sometimes hurt people. Innocent people are falsely accused or sentences don't fit the crime."

"Especially for black folks," remarked Camille.

"I've seen the dark side of people and the dark side of the law." He angled his head to look into his mother's serious eyes. "So I'm thinking about leaving my position. I have an offer to join a law firm. The fact that it handles criminal and civil cases appeals to me, but I'm not sure if that firm is the right firm for me."

"I hope you take it." Camille affectionately patted his thigh. "I always worry that you're going to convict somebody and they're going to come after you for revenge."

"That hasn't happened." Steele avoided his mother's probing stare. Not wanting to worry her, he didn't tell her that threats from convicted criminals were part of the territory. Some threats he took more seriously than others. He'd grown accustomed to that watch-your-back feeling and carried a gun like many district attorneys. But he was tired of looking over his shoulder. "If I don't work for that firm, I'm looking into other law firms. I want to be a partner."

"Well, son, my advice is take the job and go find the girl." She leaned over and kissed him on the cheek. "And you'll live happily ever after."

"Mama," he said, chuckling. "You've read too many romance novels."

"I'm going to keep reading them. I like reading about the beauty of love."

Twelve

Steele sat at the long wooden table of a conference room in the New Orleans Parish District Attorney's Office building, preparing to meet with defense attorney Jack Gould and his client Edward "Zippy" Morelli who was facing a murder charge. With a week to trial, Steele appeared calm, good-humored, because a moment earlier, he had expressed to fellow assistant district attorney Peter Schwartz that the meeting was pointless. He had absolutely no intention of offering or even considering a deal. But Jack Gould, in his usual persuasive manner, insisted on a meeting.

A soft rap on the door drew Steele's attention away from the voluminous file about the case. He looked up as Jack Gould swung open the door and came into the small décor-less room. The man reminded Steele of his favorite law school professor. Jack had wavy ginger hair and his blue-green eyes reflected the quicksilver surfaces of his moods—sometimes cold, sometimes remote, and sometimes deeply empathetic or crinkled in amusement or laughter.

"Steele McDeal," greeted Jack, warmth radiating from his mercurial eyes. "How the hell are you?"

"Fine, just fine," he answered, shaking the defense attorney's hand while observing Edward Morelli standing beside him. "Have a seat."

"Thanks." Jack took the seat across from Steele, and his client sat in the chair on his left side.

"What can I do for you?"

"Not much time for small talk," remarked Jack, more for the benefit of his client than himself. He knew that Steele was direct and forthright.

Steele gave him a sardonic smile. "I missed that class in law school."

"I'm here to talk about a deal."

Steele nodded, his face deliberately unreadable. He glanced at the man he was prosecuting for hiring the hitman who murdered Anthony Butler, a business competitor. The man he saw was heavyset, with salt-and-pepper hair, wide, perceptive eyes, and a look of keen intelligence. Dressed in a gray double-breasted suit, Edward Morelli appeared to be an ordinary American man in his thirties with a wife, two children, and a house in the suburbs. But Steele knew otherwise.

"I'd like you to consider a plea-bargain arrangement with no time."

Steele's face instantly showed incredulity. "Why would I do that?"

"Because you're a nice guy."

"I am a nice guy." Steele glanced at Edward. His face was unreadable, but there was no mistaking the anger burning in his eyes. "Your client isn't a nice guy."

"The construction business is a difficult business." Jack paused, lips working, as if he'd tasted something bitter. "Just because you're an aggressive businessman doesn't mean you're a murderer."

"In this case, it does." Steele flashed a mock smile. "We have testimony that Mr. Morelli hired Kerry Paxton to kill Anthony Butler."

"For what reason? He wasn't banging his wife."

"Mr. Butler outbid him for a construction project that he wanted."

"It wasn't the first time Butler outbid him. They're former business partners and now rivals."

"It's a rather interesting coincidence that Morelli's company gets the construction project," said Steele. "The jury might read that as motive."

"Coincidences happen."

"Motive or coincidence?" Posturing a perplexed expression, Steele held out his hands, palms up. "I prefer to let a jury decide."

"Why waste the jury's time or taxpayers' money?" countered Jack. "The only thing you have linking my client to the crime is the testimony of a known felon with numerous arrests."

"Yes, Mr. Paxton is a convicted felon. But he pulled the trigger at the behest of Mr. Morelli."

"What if the jury doesn't believe Paxton?"

"He was found with the murder weapon." His eyes veered from the defense attorney to his client. "He confessed voluntarily."

"I can paint a different picture of a confession. Make it sound like coercion," Jack said with bravado in his voice. "Especially when the detective has a reputation for getting too physical."

Steele maintained a neutral expression. "We didn't offer him a deal to testify against your client. Plus Mr. Morelli's record isn't squeaky clean."

"He had a wild period in his youth," Jack said, shrugging. "For the past five years, he's been clean."

"He just hasn't been arrested. His name has come up in other cases."

Jack shook his head, preferring not to pursue that line of conversation. Instead, he offered an alternative motive related to the victim's possible involvement in illegal dealings. "From what I understand, Mr. Butler had many enemies. Other people wanted him out of the way. In fact, my client knows about Butler's connection to the Patterson family." Pausing, Jack permitted himself a fleeting smile. "I know they're being investigated by the feds for drugs and money-laundering."

"That's not my jurisdiction." Steele's face was inscrutable.

"Hear me out first." He paused, choosing his next words with care. "My client can provide information that links Butler to the Patterson syndicate in exchange for a reduced charge and no jail time."

"I'm not interested in frying large fish."

"It could be a political feather in your cap."

Steele gave him a probing look. "I'm also not interested in politics."

"It's a simple deal. No jail time for my client and you get to take a bigger bite out of crime."

"I'm sorry, but you wasted your time." Steele rose from the table, signaling the meeting was over. "No deal."

"Thank you for your time," Morelli said, speaking for the first time. His voice had a gritty edge. Surprised, Steele looked over, fully expecting to see a pair of angry eyes. He did indeed. Morelli's eyes could have drilled holes through his. They were un-blinking, implacable, dark tunnels of rage.

Rick parked his Jaguar directly in front of his townhouse between two Lincoln Navigators. The music on the soft-rock radio station seemed to come from far away, one note at a time, as distant as his thoughts. He didn't notice that one of the SUVs was occupied. The occupants of the dark-tinted vehicle noticed Rick. The two men had been waiting for his arrival. Impatiently waiting.

Releasing the door lock, Rick pulled the door handle and swung one leg out of the car when a deep voice commanded him to "Stay in the car." Two men then got into his car; one slid into the passenger seat and the other took the rear driver's side seat. Beads of perspiration instantly clustered on Rick's face.

"Drive!" commanded the man behind him.

Without looking at the men who'd jumped into his car, Rick nervously guided his key toward the ignition. After several unsuccessful attempts, he finally inserted the key and started the engine.

"You can have the car," Rick said, assuming that he was being carjacked. "You can have my wallet . . . whatever you need," sputtered out of his mouth.

"Mr. Q. don't want your car," said the man next to him in a gruff, intimidating voice.

Sweat poured down Rick's face, his heart beat faster than a jaguar running at top speed. This was almost worse than being carjacked. Rick slowly turned his head to make eye contact with the man in the passenger seat. He had a young-looking face filled with freckles underneath a mop of red hair. Gazing into the man's eyes was like looking through a dark tunnel. His long, large frame was cramped inside the sports car's narrow passenger seat.

Looking into the mirror at the man behind him, Rick almost urinated in his pants. He wasn't as big or tall as the man in the passenger seat, but he flashed an evil smile and a large gun.

"Drive!" commanded the man to his right.

Rick shifted the car into reverse and slowly backed out of the parking spot. "Where to?" he asked, uncertain which direction to turn the wheel.

"Just drive."

His sweaty palms gripping the steering wheel, Rick applied too much gas, making the tires screech and the passengers' necks jerk back.

"Slow down," said the man next to him.

"You trying to kill us," complained the man in the back seat. He raised his gun to make sure that Rick could see it. "That's our job."

"Don't get him any more scared than he already is." Pointing, the red haired man said, "Take a left here. Besides we're not going to kill you."

"Not today, anyways." The man with the gun laughed.

Staring at the road, Rick forced himself to concentrate on driving, even though he had no idea where he was going.

"We're here on the behalf of Mr. Q," explained the red-haired man.

"Mr. Q?"

"Don't play dumb," screamed the man in the backseat.

"Mr. Quinn. The man you owe 50 big ones to."

"I'm trying to raise the money," Rick said in a quavering voice. "I just need more time."

"Mr. Quinn's a very generous and very patient man. Wouldn't you agree?"

"Yes."

"But Mr. Quinn isn't a dumb man."

"I know he isn't."

"What makes you think he don't know about you gambling . . ." he paused, before continuing, "at other establishments."

Stopped at a red light, Rick leaned over the steering wheel and shut his eyes, pondering how to respond without further endangering his life. The light turned green, but Rick didn't move forward.

"Hey, pay attention up there," said the man with the gun.

Rick jerked his head up and pressed the gas pedal. "I was trying to make some money so I can pay Mr. Quinn."

"That's not how it works Boullain boy," said the red-haired man. "First you pay Mr. Quinn, then you can gamble."

"I need more time."

"You don't have much time."

The man with the gun leaned forward and whispered, "Tick, tick, tick."

Coming to a yellow light, Rick pressed the gas instead of the brake, screeching dangerously through the intersection.

"Punk, pay attention to the road!" commanded the man beside him.

"Okay, okay," Rick said, narrowly avoiding a car

turning in his direction. "I just need some time to get the money."

"You're running out of time," said the man with the gun.

"Mr. Quinn wants his money in ten days."

Rick swallowed. "I can't raise that kind of cash in ten days," he explained, the pitch of his voice rising with each word.

"Looks like you'll have to ask your rich daddy for the money," taunted the gun-toting man.

"He won't do it," Rick said, shaking his head. "Not anymore."

"We don't care about your beef with you father. We just want the money."

"I'm trying! I'm trying!"

"I guess this time you'll have to get on your knees and ask your daddy and mommy."

Rick shook his head, his stomach burning, his thoughts churning with ways to raise the money. *How can I withdraw money from mother's account without her knowledge? Maybe I can get a loan against the deed to their house.*

"We don't care how you get the money. You can rob a bank for all we care," said the red-haired man.

"The bottom line is this: you have ten days to come up with the dough." He wrapped his finger around the gun's trigger and made a shooting sound. "Or bang, bang. You're dead."

A bolt of fear splintered down Rick's spine.

"Now, drive back to your place."

Thirteen

Isadora Graham was twenty-six years old and had the face of the beauty queen she'd once been and the body of a whore. She'd been Miss New Orleans and was second-runner up for Miss America several years ago. Her wide-spaced mermaid green eyes were bright with passion, and her mouth was sensuously pouty.

"Now, Rick, now," she urged breathlessly. "I want to feel you inside of me." She spread her legs wide in invitation.

Rick slipped on a condom, then slowly lowered himself, penetrating the petals of her blond-furred mound.

The sensation was so incredible that for a moment Isadora forgot who she was. She clamped her legs around his torso and held tight.

He slowly moved inside her, all the while kissing her on the lips, ears, eyes, neck, chin, breasts: anywhere his mouth could reach while steadily thrusting in and out, in and out.

Beneath him, she writhed and lifted her hips to meet him, dazzling sensations washing over her.

His tempo increased and she kept up the rhythm, thrashing wildly beneath him. Her head whipped back and forth, her mass of blond hair wildly flinging against the pillow.

"This is it," she cried. "Faster! Faster!"

Harder and faster he moved, his hips bucking furiously.

Then the moment they'd been waiting for came. Together they collapsed, panting breathlessly, the intensity of the orgasm reverberating through their bodies.

They lay quietly for a long while.

"That felt good," Rick said.

"Damn good," she agreed. "I need some water."

Rick got out of bed and slid into his boxer shorts before going downstairs into her kitchen for thirst-quenching relief.

Upstairs in bed, Isadora's mind was overtaken by memories she struggled to control. Memories of Rick's father in her bedroom, doing precisely the same thing: putting on his shorts before leaving the room. She was amused by their similar display of modesty. But she wasn't amused by their rejection. Rick's father was unrelenting and absolute: *I'm not leaving my wife.* This he confessed after they'd spent many hours in bed. He never wavered on his position. But Rick's rejection, she believed, was temporary, based on fear of marriage and his youth. His rejections weren't as coldly delivered as his father's. His resistance was melting and his mind slowly opening to the possibility.

His father's mind was completely opposed to the prospect of disconnecting his life from his wife and reassembling a new life with her. She couldn't find a way inside his mind to even plant the seed of possibility. Sex was her only sphere of influence; but

Richard Senior was only influenced in the heat of passion. Memories of his rejection brought unbidden tears to her eyes. With a concentrated effort, she slammed a mental door on that train of thought. Continuing along that thought path would only lead her to revisit the heartache of her life.

With the sudden taste for a cigarette, Isadora turned on her bedside lamp. She opened the nightstand drawer and retrieved a pack of Kool 100s. Searching the drawer for a cigarette lighter, she spotted her gun. It was in the wrong drawer, so she picked it up and put it in the third drawer under some folded hand towels. She found her lighter and flicked the flame on the cigarette tip, inhaling until a small light burned. With her mind on marriage, she smoked the cigarette.

Rick came into her bedroom, carrying a silver tray that contained water, whiskey, cheese, crackers, and grapes.

"That's what took you so long." She blew a cloud of smoke into the air.

"I thought you might be hungry."

"Hungry for what?" She provocatively tossed the covers off her naked body.

Staring at her voluptuously sculpted body, Rick felt his loins stir. "I need some energy because I'm not done with you."

She spread her legs and arched her hips, displaying her innermost private parts. "You want more of this."

Rick swallowed to gain control of his impulse to drop the tray and penetrate the opening between her thighs. It took all of his control to resist that urge.

A cat-like grin curved her lips as she rose from the bed. She'd gotten the response she wanted: the jutting appendage inside his shorts. Naked, she walked over and took the tray from his hand, and placed it on her nightstand. She poured water into a glass for herself and whiskey into a glass for Rick. Sipping the water, she watched him drink the whiskey. An unbidden memory burst into her mind.

"You hold your glass just like your father," said Isadora. She didn't tell him that his father had once stood in that very same spot.

Rick narrowed his eyes at her, blinded by the beauty of her naked body. "What do you mean? You know my father?"

"Of course, I've met your father. Who hasn't?" She shrugged, unflinchingly meeting his curious stare. "You hold your glass at an angle, tilted to the side. You don't hold it upright."

Rick looked at the glass in his hand. It was tilted to the left. "I guess you're right."

"That's exactly what your father does."

"I never noticed," he said, thinking about his meeting with his father earlier that week. He'd asked his father for a loan—a business loan. He was receptive to the idea, but then they argued when his father made a derogatory remark that he couldn't run a business without help from others. His father's comments that he lacked business sense stung him.

Rick gulped down the whiskey as if to wash away memories of that conversation. It didn't end the way he wanted. He didn't leave with a check for $50,000.

Rick had five more days to come up with the money. Five more days to find the nerve to tell his parents about his life-or-death debt.

"My father's always had a drink in his hand. He never hid it from me," he said, reflecting on his childhood. "I guess it's just one of many things I do like him. Is that what psychologists call modeling behavior? "

"Sugar, I don't know. I went to school to party and get a husband." She let out a harsh laugh. "Too bad he got himself killed."

"Too bad." Rick popped a hunk of cheese into his mouth.

"I think Mrs. Isadora Boullain has a nice ring to it."

The intensity of her words penetrated his intoxicated mind. Marriage. This wasn't the first time she'd mentioned marriage. Either he'd have to stop seeing her or eventually he'd find himself exchanging wedding vows with her. He didn't want to stop seeing her: she was fantastic in bed and beautiful to look at. But marriage was the last thing on his mind.

"I don't want to get married," Rick said.

"I'm going to change your mind," she said softly. "I want to get married soon."

Rick let out a weary sigh. "I'm not what you think I am," he said, hoping he could dissuade her with the reality of his financial situation. "I don't have any significant money yet."

"Yet is the operative word. Isn't your business doing well?"

"In a small way. We keep getting new clients."

"I believe you're a good businessman. You're going to make that company very successful," she said. "A few years from now, you can sell it and cash out." A wry smile was on her face as she watched her words take root. She knew from Rick Senior's derogatory comments about his son that she'd entered sensitive territory. She'd put a spin on his father's words, filling up Rick's head with confidence.

Rick hungrily swallowed every word. Grabbing her, he ground his lips against her, and pushed her down on the bed.

The Edward Morelli trial didn't last long—only two days. It didn't take long for the jury to reach a verdict—two hours. Returning to the courtroom, Steele didn't know what to expect. As the jury strolled into the jury box, he watched their faces for some indication of the direction of their decision. But their faces were unreadable.

Steele's eyes veered to the defense table. Defense attorney Jack Gould was holding a quiet conversation with his client. Jack's expression was, as usual, inscrutable, wearing the stone face he portrayed for trials. But Morelli's face showed signs of fear and anger.

While the jury was still deciding on a verdict, Jack had approached him with another offer. He claimed that the witness' testimony was not very convincing. He even noted that he'd observed some of the members of the jury yawning or making expressions of disbelief. Steele had made the same observations, but his position was unchanged.

"Think about it, Steele," Jack'd said. "You can get convictions against the big bad guys."

Steele paused, as if he were reconsidering his position. "No deal," he'd said.

Now, watching the jury take their seats, Steele wondered if he'd made the right decision. Juries were unpredictable, rendering guilty verdicts on flimsy, circumstantial cases and not guilty verdicts on cases where there was no rationale for reasonable doubt. There were many types of professionals—former lawyers, judges, and psychologists—who earned a living analyzing and predicting jury behavior. But jury behavior still remained unpredictable and unexplainable.

The jury found Morelli guilty. The moments that followed were a blur to Steele: the clerk reading the verdict; the polling of the jury; the judge setting a date for sentencing. What Steele remembered most was the way Morelli looked at him: angry, bitter, and vengeful. He'd seen that look many times, but there was something different about Morelli's look. It was the look of a mortal enemy.

Steele saw Morelli's lips move. He was mouthing words at him. He mouthed them only once. Several feet away, there was no mistaking the words formed by Morelli's lips: You're a dead man.

Rick Boullain nervously stood on the corner, shifting his weight from foot to foot. He stood out—a stranger—amidst the sex shops, liquor stores, laundry mats, and slum hotels. The street was slick with rain; a moment before, a bus filled with commuters had splashed through a puddle of water and soaked the bottom of his jeans.

Just hours ago, he was caught in the rapture of Isadora's lovemaking, blinding him with lust for that moment. But while getting dressed, they argued about marriage. He couldn't believe that she was being so insistent, but he had no interest in marrying her. Rick realized that he would have to soon end their relationship. But first he had to take care of his problem with the loan sharks.

Rick desperately needed money. Although he didn't want to borrow company funds, he'd cashed a client's check and funneled the funds into his personal account. Devon would be furious, and rightfully so, but his life was on the line. He would replace the company's money, but right now he needed to pay off his gambling debt or be killed.

A shiver of fear went through him. He was afraid of the loan sharks and the parade of unusual people carousing the streets: the homeless straggler with ragged clothing and no shoes, the woman on the corner jabbering to no one, the straggly-haired prostitute smelling of cheap perfume. Hands in his pockets, Rick felt the cool drizzle on his face and hair, and smelled the exhaust fumes of a hundred cars.

A patrol car stopped at the curb in front of him. Heart racing, he looked at the police car, hoping they wouldn't notice him. It had only stopped for a traffic light; the cop in the passenger seat gazed ahead, sipping coffee from a Styrofoam cup. Rick knew he looked out of place.

He strolled along the street looking for the right

person to approach. There was the skinny black kid who jaywalked with exaggerated languor, the Latino who darted past with an edgy urban energy, the tough-looking black girl who should be in school. Before he could decide whom to approach, a young black man wearing a designer-emblazoned sweatshirt ambled in his direction. When he made eye contact with Rick, his dark eyes were as hard as bullets.

"Looking for somethin'?"

Rick stopped, too frightened to respond or move.

"What you want down here? You stand out like a sore thumb, so you better gets what you want and get up out of here."

Rick shook his head. "Okay."

"You want some rocks?"

"No drugs," Rick said.

"What?" His tone was impatient.

"I need a gun."

The man looked around with quick, darting glances. "A piece?"

"Yeah." Rick turned his head and surveyed the scene. "A gun."

The man's eyes gleamed with suspicion. "You a cop?"

"No."

The man stared at him, unsmiling. "What kind?"

Rick shrugged. "Something small, for protection. A .32-caliber or a 9 millimeter. Something for self-defense."

"I got you," the black man said. "You got five hundred?"

"Five hundred?" Rick blurted a little too loudly.

"Don't be so loud," warned the man. "Or I'm gone."

"I have three hundred in cash."

"See that Chinese restaurant on the corner?"

Rick looked down the street, and after seeing the restaurant on the other side of the liquor store, nodded his head.

"Meet me in the bathroom in twenty minutes."

Watching the man walk away, Rick questioned his sanity. His friends and family would be shocked if they knew where he was and what he was doing. This was a situation he hoped to survive, but he would never tell anyone about his descent into gambling hell.

Fourteen

Devon stepped into Rebecca Schaffer's office. It was the smallest office on the floor, but it had a spectacular view of the Mississippi River. The office manager didn't mind that the room was crowded with a desk, two file cabinets, and a side table. Even though she could have chosen a bigger office, Rebecca enjoyed watching the paddle and pleasure boats rolling along the Mississippi River.

"Have you heard from Rick?"

"He said he had a dentist appointment and he'd be in before noon." Rebecca consulted the clock on the wall. "So, I guess he'll be here in an hour or so."

"I'm very concerned about our financial situation," Devon said. "And I want to speak to our accountants. Do you have their number?"

The young white woman batted her eyes. "I have their number but—"

"But what?"

Rebecca looked away, nervously twirling her long blond hair.

Calming his tone, he said, "But what, Rebecca?"

"Rick fired them."

"He fired our accountants!" he bellowed. "When did he do this?"

"I don't remember exactly. Maybe a month or six weeks ago."

"I don't believe this," Devon angrily said, pacing the small space in the office. "He fired the accountants and didn't tell me! I'm supposed to know this kind of stuff."

She stared at him with wordless disbelief. "I thought you knew."

His eyes smoldered with suspicion. For a moment, he wondered if Rick was sleeping with her; but she didn't fit the profile. Rick preferred beautiful women who had an exotic look, and Rebecca was a rather plain-looking woman. "Is he looking for another accounting firm?"

"I don't know," she said with a shrug.

"Do you remember seeing a check come in from Stage 3 Chemicals?"

Her head wobbled up and down in a nod of affirmation. "That was a while ago."

"I want to see our files and financial records."

Rebecca raised her eyes and looked at him with concern. "Don't be mad, but Rick took them. He said he was going to work on them from home."

"I'm not mad, I'm furious!" After a moment, Devon stood still and then expelled a deep breath. He made an apologetic gesture with his hands. "I'm sorry, Rebecca. I shouldn't be taking this out on you."

Rebecca accepted his apology with a slight nod. "Rick's been acting kind of strange."

"Very strange." His mouth puckered together

like a drawstring purse. "Let me know when he comes in. As soon as he walks in the door."

"I will," she said as Devon left her office.

Gillian checked her watch—again. It was only two o'clock in the afternoon, but the day seemed to be dragging by. Even though she planned to leave in an hour, it felt like an eighteen-hour day. Every time she checked the time, she calculated how long it was before her mother's surgery. At the moment, the doctors would be performing surgery in fourteen hours.

The clock watching and pending surgery was testing her powers of concentration. Gillian was glad that she wasn't on a photo shoot. She doubted if she had enough creative juice flowing to shoot even a simple portrait. Worry juice was flowing through her veins.

An unexpected delivery from FTD interrupted her internal dialogue. She smiled while taking the bouquet of flowers, and thanked the deliveryman for brightening her day.

But the moment she read the card, a different kind of worry entered her mind. The flowers weren't from her husband, but from annoyingly persistent Sidney Masterson.

She told the man on two separate occasions that she had no interest in spending any time with him. She couldn't understand why her simple words weren't getting through.

Gillian rushed to the front door of her studio and opened it. She was relieved that the delivery truck hadn't left. "Excuse me." She repeated, "Excuse me," in a louder voice.

"Ma'am?"

She waved for the deliveryman to come to her door, then said, "Please return these."

"You don't want them? Is there something wrong with the flowers? We can replace them if there's a problem."

"The flowers are absolutely beautiful. I just don't want them." She saw curiosity in the man's eyes. "I don't particularly care for the person who sent them."

"I see. Okay, you don't want them, so I'll take them away."

"Please do." She handed him the flowers. "Sorry for the inconvenience."

By 7:00 P.M., Devon was as mad as a lobster in a pot of boiling water. Rick never showed up at the office. He had called his home and cell numbers, but Rick never answered, nor did he return his messages. He sent several e-mails, but there was no reply from rick.boullain@webgrooves.com.

Company money was missing.

Financial files were missing.

And, Rick was missing. Or, hiding.

That's what Devon suspected. Rick was hiding for a reason, a reason that reeked of misappropriation of company money. Devon wasn't going to allow Rick to destroy the business. So, he went on a hunt for Rick.

Devon went to Rick's favorite bars. A bartender told him about a new gambling place that Rick frequented. Devon hated gambling, but decided to check it out and some other gambling places. After searching for two hours with no success, Devon decided to try his townhouse again. His heart leapt inside his chest upon spotting Rick's car several blocks away from his townhouse. He pulled into the expensive, loft-style townhouse condominium development and parked in Rick's designated spot.

Devon walked up to the door and listened for sounds of movement inside. No lights were on. He didn't hear the radio, television, or voices. He rang the doorbell several times, but Rick didn't answer the door.

Devon retrieved his cell phone from his pocket and dialed Rick's number while ringing the doorbell. Rick answered on the fourth ring.

"Rick, it's me. Let me in."

"I don't want to talk right now," Rick slurred into the phone.

"I don't care if you have a woman in there. You're not going to keep avoiding me." He pressed the doorbell. "Open the door."

"All right." Rick pressed the end button on his cell phone and stumbled down the stairs.

Moments later, Rick opened the door. He rushed Devon inside and immediately locked the door.

Devon took one look at Rick and knew that their conversation wasn't going to be very productive. He was so drunk that he bumped into the cocktail table in his own living room. But Devon was determined to get some of his questions answered.

"Come into the kitchen." Rick pushed his lips together, and tried unsuccessfully to place his index finger over his lips. "Quiet. I don't want anyone to think I'm home."

"What's going on?" Devon asked when they walked into the spacious kitchen. "You lied to me about checks coming from clients. You didn't tell me that you fired the accountants and—"

"I'm in deep doo-doo." Rick slumped down into a chair. "I owe the wrong people a lot of money. If I don't pay them back—"

"So you took money from our company?" Devon's voice thundered with indignation.

"I plan to pay it back."

"When? How?"

"I don't know." Rick hung his head in defeat. "I tried gambling to get the money back." His voice crumbled with resignation. "But I just kept getting in deeper and deeper."

"We have to end this partnership," Devon said tersely. "I'm not going to—"

"What are you talking about?" Rick raised his red-rimmed eyes to stare into his partner's eyes. "Our business is successful."

"That's what you want everyone to think." The flashing time on the microwave caught Devon's attention. The time 3:38 was incorrect, so he consulted his watch. It was 10:45, much later than he realized. "I want all the files so I can—"

"No can do." Rick shot up from the chair, and suddenly removed a gun from inside his jacket pocket. He leveled the weapon in Devon's direction.

"Whoa man!" Devon's body quaked with fear. He stepped back, his arms extended in the air. "You can't shoot me."

"I don't want to shoot you, Devon," he said in a regretful tone. "You've been a friend to me." He couldn't look at Devon and lowered the gun's aim, his mind struggling to concentrate.

Not sure what to do, Devon quietly stepped further away from Rick.

"But you're not taking my situation seriously," Rick bellowed, re-aiming the gun at Devon's chest. "I'm carrying a gun because these people want their money back and I don't have it."

"Rick, put the gun down!" Devon commanded, hoping that his abrupt tone would filter through Rick's intoxicated mind. "You really don't want to shoot me."

Wobbling on his feet, he couldn't clearly focus on Devon's face. The gun almost fell out of his hand.

"Put the gun down before you shoot yourself."

Self-preservation the stronger instinct, Rick laid the gun on the kitchen table. A strange expression descended upon his face as comprehension dawned. He picked up the gun and put it in a kitchen drawer, then dropped back down in the chair. "I'm sorry. I'm really sorry."

"You need to get some help about gambling . . . and drinking."

Rick wiped his face with his hands. "I know."

"You probably need to get the money from your father."

"I can't take all this pressure. These people want their money. Isadora keeps bugging me about marriage," Rick finally looked at Devon. "I don't want to marry her."

"Tell her you don't want to get married."

"When I told her she flipped out. She started screaming and crying and throwing things at me."

"You need to take care of your problems."

"I don't know what to do." Rick slumped over his kitchen table in a drunken stupor.

"I'm out, man," Devon said, shaking his head. The anger he felt was softened by the realization that Rick was battling against a powerful addiction. However, it was Rick's battle to fight. "This partnership is over."

Gillian's eyes flew open. Her heart was pounding as fast as if she'd been running for two miles. It was dark in her bedroom, but it had been very light in her dream—eerily light. She'd heard Nolah's voice calling her mother. "Mama, Mama, come here."

Gillian's restless sleep and sudden cry awakened Romare. He turned over and drew Gillian close to his body. He tenderly kissed her forehead. "I'm right here, baby."

She cradled her head against his shoulder. "I had a terrible dream about Nolah and Mama. Nolah was calling Mama—"

"What happened?"

"I don't know," she said. "I woke up."

"And your mother's going to wake up from surgery."

"I can't wait for this to be over."

"I know," soothed Romare. "Go back to sleep. We'll be getting up in a few more hours."

Gillian glanced at the digital glow on the bedside clock. It was three o'clock in the morning. Six hours before her mother's life-and-death surgery.

Fifteen

"You probably need to get an attorney."

Devon glanced at Brielle sitting in the passenger seat of his Honda Passport. "He had a lot of nerve taking money from the company! A lot of nerve!"

"Watch the light!" shrieked Brielle.

Devon pressed the brake pedal, stopping just as the light turned red. "I would never do anything like that." With a bitter, humorless laugh, he said, "They'd put my ass in jail."

"You have to calm down and think rationally."

He whipped the Passport into the parking lot and slammed on the brake, pitching her forward against her seat belt. "I'm going to talk to Romare. He knows about business; he's an executive. He'll give me some good advice."

"I wouldn't just close the business down and go work for someone else."

"I was talking crazy last night. Just mad and frustrated. But I'm not going to say anything to the staff until I can—"

"Assess the situation," Brielle said.

"That's a very nice way of putting it. You're pretty good at that." Devon leaned over and kissed her.

***

Inside the office suite, Devon led Brielle to his office, passing Rebecca's office along the way.

"Hey, Devon," Rebecca yelled from her office.

Devon stopped and turned into Rebecca's office.

Spotting Brielle behind Devon, Rebecca waved at her. "We got a check in the mail today from Chandler and Chandler."

"That's good news. Have you heard from Rick?"

"Not a peep."

"Okay. I'll be in my office." Looking at Brielle, he said, "I can't wait to show you what we've come up with for one of our clients. It's bad! Really, really bad!"

"I can't wait to see it."

They walked inside his office and heard, "I'm Bad," by Michael Jackson playing on the radio. "See, I'm bad! I'm bad, you really really know it!" he sang, mimicking Michael Jackson's spin-around move.

"Another old song," teased Brielle. "How old were you when that song was out?"

"I don't know." He sat at his computer and made some keystrokes and mouse clicks. "Voilà! Come over here," he said, beckoning her with his hand. "This is bad!"

"Wow! Flash animation and everything!" Brielle stared at the computer screen, amazement shining on her face. "It is bad, really really bad!" repeating the song's hook.

Devon gave her a proud smile.

"Devon Ellington!"

Devon and Brielle looked in the voice's direction, their smiles fading upon seeing two stern-faced men standing in the doorway.

An uneasy feeling spread through Devon's body. "Yes?" He glanced at Brielle before looking back at the men in the doorway. "Can I help you?"

"I'm Detective Greer and this is my partner Detective Owens."

"What can I do for you?"

Detective Greer moved inside the office. "Where were you last night between 10:30 and 11:30?"

A quiver of fear shot through Devon. "I was at my partner's townhouse."

"Mr. Ellington, step away from the desk." The detective's tone was abrasive and commanding.

He studied the detective's face. There was no mistaking the serious gleam in his eyes as a misguided joke. Devon moved from behind his desk.

"Put your hands behind your back. I'm placing you under arrest."

"What?" screeched Brielle.

Confusion reigned on Devon's face. "What? Why? I don't understand. This must be a mistake."

Detective Owens laughed. "We've heard that one before."

"Mistakes are for the courts to decide," said Detective Greer.

"Why are you doing this?" Brielle cried. "Why are you arresting him?"

"He's the number one suspect," said Detective Owens. "Heck, he's the only suspect."

Detective Greer locked handcuffs around Devon's wrists. "You're under arrest for the murder of Rick Boullain."

Devon's eyes widened. "Is Rick dead?"

"Dead as Elvis Presley," said Detective Greer.

"I didn't kill Rick!"

"You just said that you were at his house last night." Detective Owens stood toe-to-toe with Devon. "This is a slam dunk, brother," he said mockingly.

"Like I said," Detective Greer chimed in, "it's up to the courts to figure out any mistakes."

"Call my brother," he said, staring into Brielle's tear-filled eyes. "Call Romare!"

"What's his number?"

"You have to come with us, Mr. Ellington."

"I'm not resisting arrest or anything like that." Devon looked at Detective Greer. "Can I give my girlfriend my brother's number?"

The detective hesitated for a moment, then nodded his consent.

"It's 555-325-6745. Gillian's cell is 555-325-6744."

"I'll call them right now," she said, punching the numbers into her cell phone. Tears fell down her face as she watched Devon leave in handcuffs.

The doctors had informed Gillian that bypass surgery was a long and tedious process: "It can take six to eight hours." Gillian had read the brochures, but she wasn't prepared for the emotional anxiety and mind-boggling fear she'd feel while waiting to find out if her mother would survive the surgery.

She came prepared with magazines and books, but she couldn't focus her mind on the words on the page. She watched Romare typing on his laptop computer, wishing she had his powers of concentration.

The sound of her ringing cell phone almost

made her scream. She reached into her purse and retrieved the phone. She didn't recognize the number in the caller ID window and was definitely not in the mood to speak to a stranger. She showed the number to Romare. "I don't know who it is either," he said.

The phone stopped ringing and she slipped it back into her purse.

Moments later, Romare's cell phone rang.

Romare and Gillian exchanged quizzical stares.

"I think it's that same number," Romare said, before pressing the talk button. "Hello."

"Romare, it's Brielle. Devon's been arrested." The words flew out of her mouth.

"Arrested?" Romare repeated with disbelief. "Arrested for what?"

"Who's been arrested?" Gillian asked.

"Devon!" he said to Gillian, bewilderment on his face. Turning his attention back to the phone, he said, "Calm down, Brielle and tell me what's going on."

Gillian watched her husband's face as he intently listened to Brielle. She could see the muscles in his face tighten with worry.

"I'm on my way," Romare said before disconnecting the call.

"What's going on?"

"Devon's been arrested for murder."

Stunned, Gillian stared at Romare, her mouth wide open. She finally asked, "Murdering who?"

"Rick Boullain."

She covered her mouth with her hand. "Oh no!"

"I have to go, baby. I know you're worried about

your mama, but she's going to pull through. Right now, I have to see what's going on with Devon."

"I understand." She ran her hands through her braids. "This makes no sense. Devon wouldn't kill anyone."

Gillian stepped into the circle of Romare's arms and hugged him tight.

"Call me as soon as you know something," Romare said.

"I will," she promised before kissing him, "Let me know what's going on with Devon."

Sixteen

"You've got a murder case coming your way."

Steele flicked his eyes from the gleaming computer screen to the glinting gaze of assistant district attorney Peter Schwartz. Preppily-attired, as usual, Peter was the quintessential upper crust Southern male: white, ambitious, educated, and trust fund endowed. He was awkward with women, but completely at ease with lady justice, whom he called his first love. Peter somehow managed to have an inside track on major criminal investigations—local, state, and federal.

"And a little birdie told you," Steele flippantly said.

"I wouldn't be so smug. It's a doozie of a case," Peter said, taking a seat in the only uncluttered chair in Steele's cramped office. His office differed very little from other district attorneys' offices: small interior, metal desk, legal file cabinets, and two bookcases brimming with legal books. The furniture was worn and well-used; the only recent purchase was the computer perched atop his desk.

"What's the story?" Steele inquired.

"It's juicy. It's just what you need to forget about

your vacation. That's why I don't take long vacations. The recovery time is brutal."

"Get to the point, Peter."

"Rick Boullain was murdered."

"Is that so?" Steele laced his fingers together and placed them behind his head. "Did his wife finally kill him for having yet another mistress?"

"I heard he can be a mean son of a bitch. But it's the son who was murdered."

"What happened?"

"The details are sketchy. The son was shot last night. Someone—I'm not sure who—found him dead this morning in his townhouse."

"Any suspects?"

"Oh yes." He paused for effect. "He was arrested early this afternoon."

"That was unusually quick," Steele scowled. "It doesn't sound like he was standing over the body with the gun in his hand."

"Nothing's ever that easy."

Steele checked his watch. "Chances are he won't get a bond hearing today."

"You're probably right."

"Send me the file as soon as it comes in. I want to know everything there is to know before I go into the bond hearing."

"Don't have much info right now, except that the charge is murder."

"With Rick Boullain as the vic, this won't be a simple case." Steele rubbed his chin, a contemplative look on his face. "That family has such a scandalous history."

"Their last name should be scandallain," Peter joked.

Steele just shook his head. "The media is going to have a field day."

"You know that Rick Boullain, Sr. is a heavy contributor to Robert Walsh's campaign," Peter said, referring to his boss.

"I've heard. He's going to pressure this office to crucify whomever the suspect is."

"I hope the suspect isn't someone I know," Peter said.

"I hope there's real evidence to go after the suspect." Steele noticed the sudden twitch in Peter's left eye—he called it the lying eye. "They did find the gun?"

"They're looking for it."

Mentally-drained and emotionally exhausted, Gillian lay on the couch in the family room waiting to hear from Romare. It had been a grueling day. Two crises in one day: her mother in surgery and Romare's brother arrested.

Unbelievable.

At the hospital, she'd studied the doctor as he approached her in the waiting room, looking for a sign from his face of what was going to come out of his mouth: good news or bad news. The doctor's face was inscrutable.

Gillian sat on the edge of her seat, her hands clasped tightly together, her attention fully focused on the cardiac surgeon whose hands had literally touched her mother's heart.

"The surgery went well." A small smile formed on his lips. "Extremely well."

A loud sob burst from Gillian's mouth, followed by a tunnel of tears—tears of relief.

It was a momentary sense of relief.

Hours later, she was filled with anxiety over Devon's arrest. It was too unbelievable to comprehend, so she sat on the couch, mindlessly flipping the channels. Nolan and Jordy were asleep in their beds with not a care in the world. At this moment, Gillian wished she were a child.

Upon hearing the garage door open, she turned down the volume on the television. She closed her eyes and listened for voices and footsteps. Within seconds, she heard what she wanted to hear: two car doors closing and the sound of two distinct voices. Tears welled in her eyes.

Gillian rushed to greet them at the kitchen door. Before Devon could step into the house, she had wrapped her arms around his thin frame. "I'm happy to see you, boy." She searched his face and saw shadows of worry and fear. "I'm so sorry this is happening."

"Me, too." Devon went into the kitchen and headed straight for the telephone.

Engulfed in Romare's comforting arms, Gillian kept repeating, "Baby, baby, baby." Now that Romare was home, she could release the dam on her emotions. Tears ran down her face.

"It's okay," Romare said, tenderly stroking her face. "Your mom made it through surgery and Devon's here. We're going to get through this. I would have called you earlier, but my cell phone died."

Devon talked to Brielle for a few minutes, and

then interrupted Romare and Gillian. "Excuse me, do you mind if Brielle comes over?"

"Not at all," Gillian said, wiping her tears away with the back of her hand.

"She wants to see me." He paused before adding, "And I need to see her."

"It's fine with me," Romare said.

"I know you guys must be hungry—" Gillian said.

"Starving!" Devon said.

"There's plenty of pizza and wings over there." She looked at her husband. "I ordered you a shrimp po'boy and fries. I'll heat it up."

"Thanks, baby."

Food was heated up and drinks poured, and they all sat around the kitchen table. Romare and Devon had been eating for a few minutes when Gillian asked the question of the hour. "What happened? How did you get him out?"

"When I left the hospital I called Sterling."

"I didn't even think about him." She nodded her head in approval. "He was the right person to call."

"He most definitely was. With such a serious charge, I knew I had to get a lawyer right away. Sterling immediately took my call and told me to call an attorney friend of his, Ashton Jeffries. Sterling said this was going to be a very political case and that we needed a very connected and high-powered attorney."

Romare paused to gulp down some soda. "I called Mr. Jeffries. I was on hold for a few minutes, but Sterling had already called and explained the situation. Mr. Jeffries picked up the phone and said he would meet me at the courthouse. He said he had to make some calls first to get a bond hearing."

"The detectives told me that I would have to spend the night in jail." Devon blotted his mouth with a napkin. "They don't usually do bond hearings after 4:00."

"When I got to the courthouse, I was told there wasn't going to be a bond hearing," Romare explained. "All I kept thinking was I didn't want Devon to spend the night in jail. Then I was told that the chances of getting a bond on a murder charge were very slim." He cast a glance at his brother. "I was starting to feel afraid for Devon."

"I was getting nervous so I called Sterling and told him I was waiting to hear from Mr. Jeffries about a bond hearing. Sterling told me to contact a bond company so that when the bond is set, we could post bail," Romare continued.

"I know you were frantic." Gillian touched Romare's face.

"I was so scared in there." Devon closed his eyes, shuddering at the memory.

"I called a couple of bond companies, but because I didn't know the amount of the bond, they couldn't help me," Romare explained. "Finally, Mr. Jeffries called and told me the bond hearing would be at 7:00. He also put me in touch with a bond company. I went over there and did the paperwork."

"Gillian, I'm sorry," Devon said. "It's a lot of money."

"I had to put up the house." Romare's eyes connected with Gillian's. "That was the fastest way."

"I understand. We'll work it out."

"That DA was no joke. He wanted no bond at all," Devon said. "He's a brother, too."

"I know he was just doing his job, but he's tough," Romare explained. "Mr. Jeffries is an old man, but he's a feisty lawyer. He argued that Devon was being falsely accused. The police acted in haste without fully investigating the murder. He was amazing."

"He's old but can flow with that lawyerese lingo," Devon said.

"They went back and forth, but the judge ordered a $250,000 bond," explained Romare.

"This is unbelievable," Gillian softly said.

"I think Jeffries knew which judge to call and how to play it in court."

"Why do say that?" Gillian asked.

"Something Sterling said about Mr. Jeffries having to connect with the right judge."

"Thank y'all so much." Tears pooled in Devon's eyes. "I don't think I would have survived a night in jail."

"We know," Gillian said, patting his back.

"I didn't do it." Devon stopped and regained control of his emotions. "I was over there last night, but when I left Rick was alive. He was drunk, but he was alive."

"We believe you," Romare said. "You can tell us the details tomorrow when we meet with Mr. Jeffries."

"Already?" Gillian questioned.

"There's going to be a preliminary trial in three days."

"A trial?" gushed Gillian.

"It's legal strategy," Devon said.

"Mr. Jeffries thinks he can get the charges dismissed. We won't wait months and months for a trial.

This way, we can clear Devon's name and be done with it."

Gillian yawned. "I need to get some sleep,"

The doorbell rang. "I'll get it," Romare said.

Moments later, Brielle came into the kitchen and ran into Devon's outstretched arms. "I'm so happy to see you."

"Ditto," Devon said, kissing her on the lips.

"I'm sorry to come over here so late, Gillian, but I just had to see him."

"I understand. I'm very tired so I'm going up to bed. You're welcome to stay the night, Brielle. There are two guest bedrooms."

Brielle smiled in understanding and then hugged Gillian. "You are too kind. Thank you."

"We'll see you two in the morning," Romare said, taking Gillian's hand and leading her up the back stairs.

Devon moved to the foot of the stairs. "Does Tangi know?"

"I called her. I talked to Adele," Romare said, "but I haven't heard from Tangi."

Seventeen

The beauty of Bali, an island in the Pacific Ocean near Indonesia, reminded Tangi of Porta Plataea—the lush tropical gardens, the crystal white sand, the emerald ocean. Yet, it was different in many ways. Bali had a distinct culture and history. It wasn't purchased and constructed to mimic paradise in a resort-like fashion—it simply was paradise.

Still it was a tropical island reminiscent of the time spent in Porta Plataea. But a very important ingredient was missing—John Doe.

It had been almost two weeks and she still hadn't heard from him. With each passing day, she grew more curious about him and anxious to hear from him. Like an old-fashioned schoolgirl, she waited for him to make the first move. At night, her body ached for his touch and her soul longed to hear his voice.

"Cut!" was the voice she heard, reeling her from sweet reverie to the present moment. She was covered with sand from head to toe, shooting a scene in a music video in which she mysteriously rises from the sand while a popular rhythm and blues singer sits on the beach crooning about a lost love.

Tangi represented the lost love and magically appeared because of the emotion expressed in the song. She couldn't visualize the concept of the video from the script, realizing that it would take creative computer animation and filmmaking magic to actualize the concept.

This was her third music video. She'd been in two other videos, and had turned down offers to appear in several other music videos because they were usually bedroom scenes. With Adele's insistence, she agreed to appear in this music video because of the uniqueness of the project.

"We're losing light, so we'll have to finish this scene tomorrow," the bearded video director said. "Tangi, we're done with your scene for now."

"Great! I can get this sand out of my skin and hair."

"I really appreciate your fortitude." He kissed Tangi on the cheek. "You haven't complained and I know you weren't prepared to have sand swirling around you."

"I still can't imagine what it's going to look like on film."

The director laughed. "You'll look like a sand goddess wrapped in gold."

"I can't wait to see it," she said, smiling. "I'm going to my trailer and then back to my room."

Inside the trailer, Tangi closed her eyes while the make-up artist removed the layers of makeup from her face and skin.

"Excuse me," a deep voice suddenly said.

Tangi's eyes flew open. It sounded like John Doe's voice. She found herself looking into the eyes of Dean "Cricket" Waters, one of the hottest record producers with his own record label and clothing line. Cricket lived a glamorous lifestyle and had coined several terms that had become part of the hip-hop culture, often seen in newspaper and magazine articles and spoken by record industry pundits. He managed the careers of top rhythm and blues artists, hip-hop singers, and rappers. Cricket was well-known for making re-mixes of songs that became summer anthems and nightclub favorites. The video she was shooting was for one of Cricket's artists.

"Hello, Tangi," he said. "I don't think we've met before. I'm Dean Waters. Most people know me as Cricket."

"Hi."

With a glance and a nod, Cricket communicated to the make-up artist that he wanted privacy. The woman smiled, then vacated the trailer.

"I hear you're doing a great job out there." Cricket dropped into a chair. "I appreciate that you're not acting like most models."

"How is that?"

"You know what I'm talking about. Demanding, high-maintenance. You're real. I've always heard that about you. That's why I wanted you to be in this video."

Tangi arched an eyebrow. "You requested me? I thought the director requested me."

"He did." He cocked his head to the side, and laughed. "I was the one who suggested you." Cricket pointed a finger at her. "I pictured you in the scene."

"I see."

"And I thought it would be a good way to meet

you." His eyes devoured her, from the strands of her hair to the gold polish on her toenails. "We've been at some of the same parties and events, but never formally met. I'm a big fan and I wanted to meet you."

She smiled at him. Sometimes he looked handsome in pictures and on TV; other times he didn't project a very appealing image. Face to face, he was more attractive than she expected. Light brown, six feet, distinctive features, and a charming aura. "I'm flattered."

"I'd be flattered if you'd have dinner with me tonight. I want to talk to you, get to know you."

Before answering she thought about a dinner invitation she'd received not long ago. An invitation that led to intimacy—emotional and sexual. She wished it was John Doe standing there waiting for her reply. But he was back to the reality of his life and probably wrapped inside the arms of another woman.

"Will you have dinner with me?" Cricket asked.

Tilting her head, she gave him a thoughtful appraisal. "Yes, I will."

"Seven o'clock."

"Eight."

"I'll send someone for you at the hotel." Smiling, Cricket kissed her on the cheek and left.

"Why don't you come in for a night cap?" Nicole suggested when Steele parked in her driveway. They'd spent the evening at the arena watching a basketball game.

"It's late and I'm tired."

"And you could use some relief," she said, placing her hand on the zipper of his pants. She felt him stiffen. "I know what you need." Her voice was soft, suggestive.

"Don't."

"I have no illusions about this relationship." She moved her hand away from his pants. "I know I'm not the one for you."

"I never—"

"And to be perfectly frank, you're not the one for me either."

Steele was silent.

"We both know this. That's what makes this . . . liaison work. We're both getting an immediate need filled." Nicole gently stroked the back of his hand. "We've always had fun together—good sex, no stress, no strain. But you've been acting strange every since you came back."

"I know."

"That's all you can say?" She pondered his silence, then said, "You don't want to hurt my feelings."

He looked into her eyes. "No, I don't," he said, a twinge of guilt in his honesty.

"You don't have to worry about hurting my feelings." She leaned over and whispered in his ear. "All I want is some sex."

Steele laughed. "Nicole, you know what I've always liked about you? You cut right to the chase."

Tangi went over to the dressing table and picked up a tube of burnt-red lipstick. She twirled it out of the gold tube and applied it in smooth rapid strokes to her lips. While putting diamond earrings into her earlobes, she heard a knock at the door.

"Got a date?" Adele asked when Tangi opened the hotel room door.

Grinning, she said, "As a matter of fact I do."

"You look beautiful as always."

"Thank you."

"Who with?"

"Cricket Waters."

"I didn't know he was here." A smile softened Adele's stern face. A former model turned agent and manager, she knew both sides of the fashion industry. "I didn't think he was coming to the shoot until next week."

"He's here." Tangi shrugged. "I'm having dinner with him."

"Be careful." Adele sat on the sofa. "He's got that bad boy image and a reputation for being a ladies' man."

"It's just one date," she quipped. "A diversion. Maybe he can take my mind off my mystery man."

"Just call the man." Adele flicked her hand back and forth in a sweeping motion. "So what? You set the rules." She laughed harshly. "Hell, you're Tangi Ellington; you can change them."

"I was seriously thinking about calling him tonight. You know, throw caution to the wind like I did in Porta Plataea."

"Tangi, please come sit down with me." Adele's expression turned grim. "There's something I need to tell you."

Tangi's face became equally grim. She slid into the chair opposite Adele. "What's going on?"

"I have some rather disturbing news."

"What is it? Has someone been hurt or in an accident?" she asked, fear and impatience in her voice.

"No, nothing quite like that." Adele squeezed Tangi's hand, and gently said, "Devon was arrested."

"Oh no! Oh no!"

"Want me to fix you a drink?"

Tangi nodded. "What happened?"

"He was arrested at his office." Adele dropped some ice cubes in a goblet-shaped glass before pouring brandy inside. "He's been accused of killing his business partner."

Tangi took the glass from Adele and sipped the brandy. "I have to go see Devon." She took a deep breath. "Is he in . . . jail? " Her heart broke apart like an eggshell at the thought of Devon behind bars.

"Romare got him out on Tuesday."

"This happened two days ago?" Disbelief rang in her voice.

"Yes."

Anger and indignation gleamed in her eyes. "And you didn't tell me?"

Adele's lips disappeared into a tight seam. "You were in the middle of a scene and I didn't want to interrupt the shoot."

Tangi jumped up from the chair. "I can't believe you didn't tell me that my brother was arrested! You know how close I am to my family. You know they mean the world to me." She stared at Adele for several moments, wondering if she was overreacting. In a word, she felt betrayed. "I've always told you to put their calls through. If I'm busy, you're supposed to give me their messages right away. You're not to screen their calls."

Adele flinched at the venom in Tangi's voice. "I didn't think you'd be this upset, Tangi. I apologize and—"

"Apology accepted." Tangi went to the door and opened it. She didn't notice Cricket Waters standing in front of the door. "You're fired."

Adele froze. "What?"

"You're fired," Tangi quietly said.

Adele stammered, "Tangi . . . calm down. I think you're . . . overreacting."

"You overstepped your boundaries, Adele. You kept important information about my family from me. I don't appreciate it and I will not tolerate it." Tangi's eyes narrowed to slits. "So, I'm asking you to please leave. You no longer work for me."

Adele was taken aback. "Tangi!"

"Now!"

"Excuse me," Cricket said, coming into the room. "I believe she asked you to leave."

Adele stormed out of the room.

Moments passed before Tangi spoke. "I'm sorry you had to witness that. I don't usually act like that."

"I don't know why you did it, but it was a turn on." His attempt to tease her failed. A quiet moment went by, broken by his question, "What happened?"

"My brother was arrested two days ago and she just now told me!" she said indignantly. "It has to be some kind of crazy mistake because my brother is straight up. He's not a thug; he doesn't hustle or do drugs. He gets high off of computer technology."

"He stays out of trouble," Cricket said.

"She knows I'm tight with my family, but she was concerned that I'd leave right away."

"And that's what you intend to do."

She glanced at him, a try-and-stop me look on her face. "Precisely."

"It's gonna cost me a lot of money to shut down this shoot."

"The director said he was almost done shooting my scenes."

"You want to see your brother." It was a statement, not a question.

"I'm going to see my brother," Tangi firmly said.

"When do you want to leave? I'll have a plane ready to take you where ever you need to go."

Eighteen

Ashton Jeffries' law office was located within walking distance of the courthouse, which towered in the background, white and imposing amid the trees that surrounded it. The law firm handled everything from high-profile criminal cases to corporate litigation involving tens of millions of dollars. Money wasn't at risk for Devon Ellington, only something more precious—his life.

"Their case is thinner than the hair on the top of my head," said Ashton, rubbing the top of his balding white head. Trading stares with Romare and Devon, he said, "Not much up there."

Sitting in the attorney's office, decorated in ornate Louis XVI-style furniture, Romare and Devon exchanged worried glances. The thin, elderly gentleman was calmly searching for something, but they didn't know what.

"Oh, there they are," Ashton said, upon finding his wire-framed glasses in the opened top drawer of his desk. Sliding the glasses over the bridge of his nose, Ashton leaned back in his chair and studied Devon. He considered himself to be a good judge of character, relying on his own gut instincts about a person. As an attorney, he'd seen the good and evil side of human behavior and was rarely surprised by a person's dark side.

Ashton's face was wrinkled and weathered, ravaged by time and the blistering sun. Intelligent blue eyes twinkled at them from sockets radiating lines of friendliness. A boisterous voice bellowed from the man's thin body.

"You're basically a good kid," Ashton finally said.

Devon scrunched his brows together. "I'm not a kid!"

"I'm pushing sixty-five. I have grandkids almost older than you, so don't be offended."

Devon inclined his head in acknowledgement of Ashton's comment.

"So, what do you think of the charges against him?" Romare asked.

"They're skating on thin ice with what they have so far. They jumped the gun before they had a chance to investigate." He retrieved an old-fashioned tape recorder from a desk drawer and placed it on top of his desk. "The problem is now that they've made an arrest, they want to prove they were right."

"Doesn't it matter that I'm innocent?" His stomach was burning in the center of his gut. Ever since the arrest it felt as if a meteor had crashed inside his stomach.

"Yes and no. Yes, if I can prove you didn't do it, and no, if they can prove you did." Ashton inserted a blank cassette tape into the recorder. His serious blue eyes met Devon's worried ones. "I will, of course, prove you didn't murder Mr. Boullain."

"Of course?" quipped Romare. "That's a rather confident statement."

"I rarely lose, Mr. Ellington. It's been eight years

since I've lost a case, and I prefer to stay on course with my winning streak."

"That's good to know," Devon said, a slight smile on his face.

"Let's start with you describing the events that occurred on Monday night." His hand poised over the record button, Ashton said, "If you don't mind I'm going to record our conversation. My secretary will transcribe it, but I'll listen to it again several times."

"Why?"

"So I can catch the details in your story, the nuances in your voice, and anything the DA will use against you. It's the details, my young man, that make the difference between winning and losing."

"What about the fact that Rick's father is a rather influential man in town?" Romare asked.

"The Boullain family will put pressure on the DA's office to find their son's murderer."

Devon lurched from his seat. "I'm not a murderer!"

"Calm down, Mr. Ellington. I'm not suggesting that you are." His tone was earnest and sincere. "I'm on your side, son."

Romare brushed Devon's arm. "Sit down," he said calmly.

Dropping back down in his chair, Devon took a quiet moment to collect himself. "I'm listening."

"The fact of the matter is the Boullain family will pressure the DA's office. Since the police arrested you, they're going to press them to get a conviction."

"I've had dinner at Mr. Boullain's house." With a heavy sigh, Devon shook his head. "I can't believe he thinks I killed Rick."

"People believe what's convenient for them to

believe. It's more convenient to believe that you did
it than to go after the skeletons in Boullain's closet:
drinking, gambling debts, money problems,
women." He gave a noncommittal grunt. "It's more
convenient—"

"To blame a black man," Romare said. It was an
uncomfortable statement to make, but was
nonetheless mixed in with the morass of legal, social, and political entanglements Devon was facing.

"You are correct, Mr. Ellington." The attorney
looked at his client. "This is the South. Need I say
more?"

"I've tried hard to stay on the right side of the
law," Devon said.

"I know, but sometimes lady justice . . . is no lady,
if you get my meaning."

An awkward silence followed his statement.

"Tell me everything you did that day from the very
beginning," Ashton finally said. "Leave nothing out."
His long bony finger pressed the record button.

The spindles spun slowly around as Devon
described the night that led to his legal predicament—the night that had become a nightmare,
only he was awake and living it. Ashton periodically
interrupted, sometimes requesting Devon to repeat
what he had said, sometimes inquiring about a
seemingly innocuous detail, sometimes asking him
to describe something about Rick Boullain.

Romare watched the lawyer as he conducted the
interview. His eyes were closed, listening as Devon
talked. He'd open his eyes when he had a question
or needed to probe for further information. He'd
also study Devon's face, searching for something
unseen.

"Have you ever met Isadora?" Ashton asked after Devon mentioned the woman's name.

Scowling, Devon shook his head. "Rick wasn't exactly the relationship type. I remember her name because he rarely mentioned a woman by name." He grimaced as a burning sensation surged through his stomach. "He joked that she wanted to get married but he wasn't thinking about marrying her."

"Were you surprised when he pulled a gun on you?"

"Shocked!" Devon flinched with bafflement. "I couldn't believe it!"

"You said he'd been acting erratic, missing appointments, not returning calls, taking money from the business. With that type of behavior, why were you surprised that he had a gun?"

"Rick had never been violent with me. I've never seen him violent with anyone. We had disagreements about the business, but it never was out of control."

"What kind of disagreements?"

"He wanted to bring investors in so that we'd have more capital to grow the business. But I didn't agree." Devon glanced at Romare then Ashton. "We agreed to disagree on that."

"How were you able to talk him into putting the gun down?"

"He was drunk and stumbling around. He couldn't hold the gun straight. I told him that he was going to end up shooting himself, so he put the gun on the kitchen table and then he put it in the drawer."

"Did you touch the gun?"

"No. He mumbled an apology and I wasted no

time getting out of there. I told him our partnership was over and left."

"Did he lock the door behind you?"

"I don't know," Devon said, shrugging. "He was in the kitchen when I left. I rushed to get out of there before he decided to pick up that gun again."

"Telling him that you wanted out of the business upset him," probed Ashton. "That's what made him pull out his gun?"

"He pullled out the gun when I told him I wanted the files." Devon leaned forward. "I didn't want to be in business with someone who took money from the business and I could no longer trust."

"That's what the prosecution will use against you. You wanted out of the business—that was your motive. You had opportunity—you were in his apartment."

"It's all circumstantial, Mr. Jeffries." Worry claimed Romare's face.

"That's my job to prove, Mr. Ellington. And rest assured, I will."

"I never even touched the gun."

"That's why we'll present evidence that you haven't fired a gun recently."

"Did they find the gun?" asked Romare.

Ashton shook his head. "The fact that they don't have the gun will work in our favor."

"That DA was aggressive in the bond hearing," Devon said.

"Steele McDeal is one of the best DA's over there."

"That's not very comforting," said Romare.

"Don't you worry, Mr. Ellington." Ashton removed his glasses. "I've been practicing law for over forty years. I already have a PI conducting our own investigation."

Ashton paused to draw a breath and rubbed the top of his head. "I don't trust the DA's office to be one hundred percent forthcoming with discovery since they don't want egg on their faces. The trick is to find someone else who had motive and opportunity." Ashton looked at the two brothers, a confident smile on his face. "And the gun."

"I can't believe there's going to be a trial on this thing," said detective Charlie Owens.

"Charlie, it's not the actual trial," said David Greer, giving his partner an impatient look.

Steele observed the exchange between the two detectives sitting in front of his desk. Instead of the good cop-bad cop dynamic, it was smart cop-dumb cop. And Charlie wasn't the smart cop. "It's a preliminary trial," Steele explained. "Preliminary trials are used to find out if there's enough evidence to hold a suspect. If not, the charges are dropped. We usually don't like prelims."

Charlie looked at Steele and David, confusion still on his face. "I know. I know. I mean I can't believe there's going to be one. I thought this case wouldn't go to trial for months."

"Ordinarily it would go to a grand jury for indictment and then there would be a trial. That takes a while. Sometimes months, even years. But Mr. Jeffries knew exactly what he was doing when he requested the prelim. And he made the request to Judge Whitaker."

"So the attorney and judge are what you call friends." A flash of light beamed in Charlie's eyes. "Are they homos?"

"I wasn't suggesting anything of that nature," Steele explained, a worried frown on his face. He wasn't going to put Charlie on the witness stand. "I mean it was a strategic move. He called in some favors and knew that Whitaker was a more liberal judge. Another judge would have denied bail and the prelim."

"Oh," Charlie said.

Steele wondered if Charlie really understood. He directed his question to David. "Tell me what happened. How did you conduct the investigation? How you were able to conclude that Devon Ellington was a suspect?"

"It was a slam dunk. One of the neighbors IDed his car," Charlie said, smiling.

"The neighbor called him by name. Apparently he'd met Devon Ellington before, so he recognized the car." David flipped out his little notebook.

"Adam Haque," said Charlie. "That's the neighbor's name."

"Yeah, he lives right next to the vic. He heard the suspect banging on the victim's door, and then he heard them arguing."

"Did he hear the gunshot?" He looked from Charlie to David. "Why didn't he call 911?"

Charlie shook his head. "He didn't hear the gunshot. He said he took a shower and went to bed."

"Did he hear anything before he went to bed?"

"We asked him that," Charlie interjected.

"He didn't hear anything. He took a sleeping pill and went to bed."

"A sleeping pill?" Steele probed.

"I didn't ask why," David said, shrugging.

"Does the witness know when Mr. Ellington left?"

"No," answered David. "But we can place him at the scene and they were arguing loudly."

Steele made notations on a yellow legal pad. "What did they argue about?"

"Rick Boullain was taking money from the business."

"How do you know this?"

"We talked to the office manager." David turned some pages in his note pad. "Her name is Rebecca Schaffer."

"Did you talk to her before or after you arrested Mr. Ellington?"

"After," David said, shrugging. "But, it made sense. That was his motive. We pulled the lugs on his phone. He made numerous calls to Rick's home and cell phone on the night in question." David handed the lug sheet to Steele.

"And you knew this before or after the arrest?"

Charlie looked at David before answering the question. "After."

"And the gun still hasn't been located?"

"We searched Devon's apartment and his girl-friend's apartment, but no gun."

Steele reviewed the lug sheet. "There are repeat calls from other numbers. Did you investigate these calls?"

Charlie shook his head.

"Why not?"

"We kind of heard that he had a big gambling debt."

"That's all the more reason to trace these calls."

David plowed his hand through his blond hair. "We got our man."

"What about the women in his life?" Steele asked.

Charlie shrugged.

"Don't know," said David.

"Detectives, we don't have much here."

"You're not trying to convict him at the prelim," said David. "You just gotta prove he's a suspect, right?"

"That's the danger of a prelim trial. You have to show that you will be able to convict," explained Steele. "From what we have so far, it's going to be difficult to convince a judge that we have enough supporting evidence." His fingers were steepled over his nose and mouth. "We have to convince a judge, not a jury."

"Man, I thought this was a slam dunk," said Charlie.

"Me, too," echoed David.

"Listen up," Steele said. "I want you to go back to his apartment and canvass the neighbors. Find out if anyone else heard what the neighbor heard. Find out if Rick Boullain had other visitors that night."

"Before or after the suspect?" Charlie asked.

Steele glared at Charlie. He couldn't believe this man was a detective. "Find out if anyone else visited the vic before or after Ellington left. Find out if anyone else can corroborate the neighbor's story." He divided his gaze between the two detectives. "And search the surrounding area for the gun."

Charlie stood up. "We'll get right on it."

"We'll let you know right away what we find out," David said before leaving Steele's office.

Nineteen

Jeremy Benson rang the doorbell to his son's penthouse apartment and hoped Steele would let him in. Clutching a legal-sized file in his hand, he rang the doorbell several times, and was turning away when the door finally swung open.

"Pops?"

"Yeah, it's me son."

His father grinned at him, emphasizing the lines in his face. Jeremy looked every day of his fifty-five years, mostly spent as a musician and singer. He was tall, chocolate-toned, big, and had a burly laugh. Still handsome, Jeremy had an eye for women, especially younger women.

Steele stood in the doorway. It was late, his father's appearance unexpected, and their visits were often framed with awkward moments.

Jeremy spread out his arms. "Give your old man a hug."

Steele embraced his father. "Come in."

"I know you weren't expecting me."

"I was up working. Want something to drink?"

"I'll take some whiskey," he said, going into Steele's office.

Minutes later, Steele came into his office. He

handed a glass of whiskey to his father who was admiring the painting of Jane.

"Ooo, wee! That's a pretty woman."

Steele shook his head, not the least bit surprised at the gleam in his father's eye. He stared at Jane, amazed that he still felt the same longing for her. Instead of dissipating, it intensified.

"That's what I do now," Jeremy said, interrupting Steele's reflections. "I mostly paint abstracts and landscapes. The woman I stay with paints, too. We got something in common."

"I didn't know you painted." Steele looked at his father, a half smile on his face. "I painted the picture."

Jeremy's eyes widened. "You kidding me, right?"

"No, Pops."

"Well, glory be." Jeremy slapped his son on the back. "We got something in common, too."

"I guess we do," Steele murmured.

"I didn't come over to talk about painting." Jeremy went over to the sofa and plopped down. "I came to see if you would help me win my case."

Steele sat next to his father. "What kind of case?"

"I've been fighting my record company for a long time. They owe me a lot of money." Jeremy whistled. "A whole lot of money."

"You're suing them?"

"Hell, yes. This case been going to court for years, but their smart-ass lawyers always find a way to stall. One time they even had my case dismissed."

"Why?"

"The lawyer I had messed up the paperwork. He didn't know what he was doing. So I got a new lawyer. Every time we got ready to duke it out in court something would happen." Jeremy gulped down some whiskey. "This last here time, my lawyer died on me."

"I'm not an entertainment lawyer."

"You know more about the law than I do. I betcha you can look at this paperwork and understand how they screwed me out of my royalties."

Steele pondered his father's request. "Let me see what you have."

Jeremy grinned like a crocodile, and handed the file to Steele. "These young cats are sampling from my music and I ain't getting a dime."

Steele drew his brows together. "You're not?"

"Not a dime." Juggling his empty glass, he said, "I'm going to fix myself another drink."

"Help yourself." Steele skimmed through the paperwork, consisting of copies of his father's original contract and various court documents. He immediately spotted flaws in the contract, flaws that resulted in the record company retaining certain rights. The contract would be unacceptable to today's wave of business-minded artists and entertainers.

When his father returned, he said, "There are a lot of things wrong with this contract."

"I didn't have a lawyer look at it. Back then, I was just happy to get a record deal."

"This contract is set up so that the record company basically owns all your recording rights."

Jeremy swallowed some whiskey. "That's why I couldn't get a record deal with any other company."

Steele shook his head. "I've heard about record companies ripping off a lot of black entertainers, especially in the 50's and 60's."

"I've been double screwed. I didn't get paid for the songs I wrote. My name isn't even listed as the songwriter. I ain't never got one red cent." Jeremy gulped down the rest of his whiskey. "Now those young cats are sampling some of my music. Every time I hear my music on the radio, some rapper cursing to my music, I just want to scream!"

Jeremy paused, closed his eyes, and reigned in his temper. "I know I ain't been much of a father to you. I helped your mother when I could. I know she struggled. But I was struggling, too. What can I say? All that glitters isn't gold? I had gold albums, but I never had no money."

They were silent for a while. In the silence, something unusual occurred. A connection was made between father and son.

"You paint real good," Jeremy finally said, staring at the painting of Jane. "Umh, umh, she sure is a pretty young thing."

"She's my friend," Steele said, his tone serious and protective. In the corner of his mind he heard himself whisper, "And I love her." But those words had yet to fully penetrate his consiousness. "A very good friend."

"Oh, that kind of friend," Jeremy said. "Maybe I'll meet her one day."

"You will." Those words escaped from Steele's mouth unbidden. At the moment, Steele realized that he had to find out who she was; he had to contact her. Something in his soul was directing him to do so.

Jeremy tapped his son's shoulder, drawing Steele's attention back to him. "Would you help me duke it out in court?"

* * *

"Mama, I'm so happy to see you sitting up in bed looking like yourself." Smiling, Gillian fingered her mother's cottony-soft gray hair.

"I'm feeling better. Don't you think the doctor should be letting me out of this place?"

"You just had major surgery. What makes you think the doctor is going to release you so quickly?"

"'Cause I'm ready to go!" Ruth stared at her daughter with a look that challenged her to dispute her.

"If they release you too soon, you might be coming back here sooner than you want to," Gillian admonished. It felt good to fuss at her mother; it meant that her mother was well on the way to recovery.

"I'm not coming back here," Ruth declared as she vigorously shook her head. "All they want to do is poke you with needles and take your blood. They're a bunch of vampires."

"All right, Mama. Don't get yourself all worked up. You don't want these monitors going off and the doctors to have to come rushing in here."

"I wasn't particularly fond of doctors before, but now I really don't like them."

"Mama, they saved your life."

She pursed her lips together. "I guess I should be grateful."

"You should!" Gillian planted a kiss on her mother's forehead. "I am."

"You know I am. That's why I got a hankering to get out of here." Ruth released a frustrated sigh and changed the topic of conversation. "When are you going to bring my grandbabies? I want to see both of them."

"I was going to surprise you, but the doctor said I can bring them on Friday."

Ruby clapped her hands in joy. "Both of them?"

"Yes, Mama."

"I can't wait to see them."

"Mama, you sound like your old self!" Mikey chimed in, his appearance surprising them both.

"Come here, son." Ruth beckoned him with her hand.

A wide grin on his face, Mikey strode over and gingerly hugged his mother. "I'm so glad you're okay." He dramatically wiped his brow. "What a relief!"

Ruby and Gillian exchanged glances. They both caught a whiff of alcohol on Mikey's breath. Neither said a word about it; it wasn't anything new, nor did chiding Mikey about his drinking change his behavior. Besides, Ruby's recovery was cause for celebration. Why ruin the moment.

"Hey, Gillian." He lightly scrubbed her jaw with his callused knuckles. "Where are the kids?"

"At home."

"She's bringing them to see me on Friday." Ruby's eyes gleamed with joyful anticipation.

"Mama, do you still miss Nolah?"

Ruby and Gillian sent bewildered looks in Mikey's direction. It was such an out of the blue question.

"Yes, I do," Ruby said fervently.

"I miss her at lot," Gillian said, feeling a sudden surge of sadness. "I can't stop thinking about her, and Jordy reminds me so much of her."

"I think about her, too," said Mikey.

The room grew silent, the beeping noise of the monitors the only sound.

"I heard Devon got arrested," Mikey said, breaking the silence in an unexpected way. "What's up with that?"

Ruby's head snapped up. "Arrested? Romare's brother?"

Gillian narrowed angry eyes at Mikey. She didn't want her mother to know about the situation.

Catching Gillian's angry gaze, Mikey stammered an apology. "I'm sorry . . . I didn't know . . . it was a secret."

"It's not a secret. I just didn't want Mama to worry."

Mikey slumped down into a chair. "I guess I messed up again."

A deep crease in her brow, Ruby's eyes veered from Mikey to Gillian. "Would someone tell me what's going on?"

Gillian briefly explained the circumstances surrounding Devon's arrest. She didn't disclose the details, but revealed the highlights, concluding with the preliminary trial that was scheduled for the next day.

"They done lost their mind. Anybody can look at Devon and tell he wouldn't hurt anybody."

"That Boullain family got clout," Mikey said. "They gotta find someone to blame. So they stuck Devon." He shook his head. "Unlucky brother."

"Romare hired a lawyer. He's supposed to be the best in town," Gillian explained. "Sterling recommended him."

"Jordy's father would know," Ruby nodded approvingly.

"He doesn't think they have much of a case against Devon." Gillian exhaled deeply. "We're on pins and needles."

"I'm going to pray for him. Pray for the whole family to get through this crisis." Ruby squeezed her daughter's hand. "You're going to make it through this."

"Tangi's coming in for the trial. I mean the preliminary trial. She'll be here in the morning."

"She's a real nice girl. Loyal to her family," remarked Ruby. "

"She's cool and the gang," Mikey said. "And she's fine as wine."

"I just talked to her a little while ago," Gillian said. "She was very upset because her agent didn't tell her about Devon until today. I thought it was strange when she didn't call right away. I knew there had to be a reason."

"Are you picking her up from the airport?" Mikey asked.

"It'll be too hectic. She's going to come to the courthouse straight from the airport."

Twenty

Life can change so quickly, so unexpectedly.

Stretched across the limousine sofa, while the limo driver navigated the fastest route to the New Orleans Courthouse, Tangi pondered the statement she'd heard many times. She'd debated the axiom in a philosophy class and had experienced the truth of that statement when she lost her parents. So quickly, so unexpectedly. A photo shoot and a phone call from a top modeling agency had changed her life. So quickly, so unexpectedly.

With an arrest for a murder he didn't commit, her brother's life could forever change. So quickly, so unexpectedly.

Tangi closed her eyes, struggling to contain the fear in her heart for her brother. Another feeling maneuvered its way from her heart to her mind as her thoughts turned to John. Spending time with him had changed her life. So quickly, so unexpectedly. A realization crept through her mind: something good happened in Porta Plataea—so quickly, so unexpectedly. Something too good to let it slip away.

Tangi decided to call John after the trial.

At the moment, she picked up her cell phone

and called Romare. "What's the courtroom number?"

"503. Fifth floor."

"Okay, I should be there in twenty minutes. Devon knows I'm coming, right?"

"He knows."

"Please don't let Devon go to jail," she suddenly cried, tears springing in her eyes.

Romare closed his eyes; he felt the same fear. "Tangi, honey, I hired the best attorney in town."

"Maybe we need to hire a famous attorney like Johnnie Cochran. I'll pay his legal fees. I don't care how much it costs."

"I've already thought about that. If we don't win this preliminary trial, then we'll get a high-profile lawyer," Romare explained. "I'm really hoping that this attorney gets the charges dropped today."

"What are the chances? Ninety percent, eighty percent—"

"Mr. Jeffries won't give odds like that. He thinks he can win. He says he hasn't lost a case in eight years and he's not planning on losing this one."

Tangi released a deep breath. "That makes me feel a little better. But I'm still scared."

"I know, honey. Pull yourself together," Romare advised. "You can't come into the courtroom looking afraid."

"Okay, big brother. See you shortly."

Wanting to be discreet and cautious, Tangi directed the limo driver to park a block from the courthouse. She departed from the limousine wearing a full-skirted black dress that floated around her slender body as she walked. A wide-brimmed black hat and dark shades concealed her identity. Five minutes later, she treaded up the courthouse steps into the building where her brother's future would be decided.

Tangi stepped into the elevator and pressed the button for the fifth floor. The elevator stopped on the first floor for a passenger that made her heart descend into her stomach.

"John!"

Steele stared at the lone woman in the elevator. Her voice brought back memories that haunted him. "Jane?"

Tangi removed her glasses. "Yes, it's me."

Steele immediately pressed the stop button on the elevator control panel. He felt the same rush of passion he'd experienced in Porta Plataea. His eyes raked over her body with unbridled lust. He wanted to undress her, gaze at her exquisite figure, and make love to her.

But now was not the time. He was due in court in fifteen minutes.

"I've missed you." He touched her face to verify that she wasn't a mirage. "When you left the island, you took the sun with you."

The beauty of his words and the tender way he spoke them made her heart swell with unexplainable joy. "I've missed you, too." She smiled at him. "And I was just thinking about you."

"I can't stop thinking about you." Steele lowered his head and kissed her softly.

"My heart is beating so fast," she said, when he released his lips from hers. "Something happened in Porta Plataea. Something beautiful and magical."

"Something that's better than a fantasy."

Her lips parted, but she couldn't find the words to express what she felt in her heart.

"Something we don't have to leave in Porta Plataea," Steele said.

They stared into each other's eyes. The longer they stared, the deeper they searched within the tunnels of their heart, discovering the same thing—love.

"The elevator must be stuck," someone complained. The loud voice snapped them back to reality.

Steele released the stop button, and seconds later, the elevator began to rise. He consulted his watch. "I have to go."

"So do I."

Suddenly curious, he asked, "What are you doing here?"

Sadness took over her face. "Too complicated to explain right now."

The elevator slowed, and loudly screeched before stopping on the third floor. "I'll call you," she promised as the doors began to open.

Nodding, Steele stepped out of the elevator. He spun back around. "What's your real name?"

Before she could answer, the elevator doors slammed together.

Tangi forced thoughts of John Doe from her mind when she opened the courtroom door. It was difficult to do. He'd been ever present in her thoughts from their first meeting. She couldn't completely exorcise him from her mind, so she pushed him into a corner of her mind, consoled by the realization that their alias name game was coming to an end. Reality would meet fantasy when they revealed their true identities. They'd be free to put a name on the emotion that claimed their hearts in Porta Plataea.

Buoyed by her conversation with John, she entered the courtroom with a heart full of hope—hope that her brother would be set free today.

She immediately saw her family, sitting in the front row behind the defense table, and rushed over to Devon. She hugged him tightly.

"I'm so sorry this is happening, Devon," she said, sounding more frantic than she intended. "I would have been here sooner if I had known."

"I know. I'm just glad you're here right now."

Tangi ran her hand across his cheeks and under his chin. "You shaved your beard. I'd forgotten what you looked like without your beard."

"It's part of the strategy," he said. "An innocent look."

"You look very handsome," said Tangi. "Hello, Brielle."

Brielle gave a half smile. "Hi."

Tangi turned toward Romare and Gillian. "Hey, you two."

"You didn't break any air traffic laws trying to get here?" Romare asked.

Gillian squeezed Tangi's hand. "She probably did."

"I wasn't flying the plane," quipped Tangi.

"You must be Tangi," Ashton Jeffries said, offering a handshake.

Tangi shook his hand. "Yes, I'm the little sister."

"I'm glad you're here." His blue eyes quickly assessed her. "You're part of my strategy."

She blanched. "I am?"

"Don't worry about it. We're going to get your brother out of this mess." He patted her on the back. "It's a mess, all right. But it's not his mess." Ashton walked back around to the defense table.

Tangi gave Romare and Gillian a skeptical look.

"He's quirky, but he's good," Romare said. "Jordy's father recommended him."

"Speaking of Sterling," Gillian said, tilting her head toward the back of the courtroom, "he just walked in." Her eyes went from Tangi to Romare. "I didn't know he was coming."

"His presence," Romare said, "will help Devon."

With court proceedings set to begin in five minutes, Steele rushed into the courtroom, his boss' words ringing in his head: *We must win this.* But Steele had explained to his boss that the case against Devon Ellington was weak. The two detectives were inept and more time was needed to thoroughly investigate the murder. Robert Walsh didn't dispute Steele's position, but he had his own agenda. He expected Steele to convince the judge that the charges against the suspect should stand. The lead district attorney wasn't as concerned about the merits of the case as he was about the merits of his political career.

"I'm not going to be a pawn," Steele had said.

"You need to win this case," Robert said bluntly. "It's that simple."

"It's not simple. It's never simple," he said with a

determined jut of his cleft chin. "I don't appreciate the position of having a black district attorney prosecute this case. You want to send the message that he must be guilty if his own kind is prosecuting him." Frowning, he gave his boss a slow, measured stare. "I've fought with you on this before, and I won't let myself be exploited, especially when there's no evidence."

"Win this," Robert ordered. "We'll get the evidence."

There was no more time to continue the conversation, so Steele jetted up two flights of stairs and entered the courtroom. He didn't look in the direction of the defense, his eyes focused on the prosecution side of the courtroom.

"Robert was just giving me his you-must-win speech," he said to his co-chair Peter, who was sitting at the long narrow table.

Peter flashed a mock smile. "What a surprise."

"Anything else that we didn't discuss earlier? Did the detectives find out—"

"We missed something very important," Peter said. "The suspect's sister is a model. A very famous model." He paused for effect. "And she's rich."

"Which weakens our motive." A grim expression on his face, Steele slumped into the chair, pondering how to reposition their case.

"She's beautiful, too." Peter nudged Steele's arm. "Look at her."

"She's here?" A sudden uneasy feeling crept through his veins. He swiveled his head, and saw Jane sitting next to the suspect. He felt the muscles in his heart contract.

Amidst the crowded courtroom and hushed conversations, Steele and Tangi made eye contact. Her confused eyes met his shocked ones.

Comprehension reigned on his face. *She's a famous model. That's why she didn't want to tell me who she is.* "What's her name?" Steele asked.

"Tangi Ellington," said Peter.

Steele glanced at her again. Her expression had changed—hurt and betrayal was on her face. In that glimpse, he knew that he loved her. He wanted to erase the pain on her face.

"All rise," the bailiff suddenly announced. "This court is now in session."

Twenty-one

"We're not here today to determine Devon Ellington's guilt or innocence. That is, of course, for a jury to decide." Steele stood in front of the table, a few feet away from the judge. "We're here to decide whether Mr. Ellington should be considered a suspect in the tragic murder of Mr. Rick Boullain. It's the people's contention that, in fact, Mr. Ellington is the prime suspect." Steele turned and made direct eye contract with Devon. When he looked away, he inadvertently caught Tangi's gaze. They stared at each other for a moment, before he broke contact.

Judge Whitaker cast an impatient look at Steele, his hands folded together on top of his desk. The black robe might have hid the bulk of his burly frame, but it didn't hide that fact that he was a big man. His large hands and wide head were visual indicators of a man whose clothing came from a big and tall man's store.

"Your Honor, this is a rather unusual case. The fact that we are here today reflects the unusualness of this situation. Ordinarily, we'd have time to launch a more thorough investigation in order to present compelling evidence to the grand jury for indictment. We haven't had time to do so."

Steele continued, "Yet I will not waste the court's time with conjecture and speculation. I will not discuss different scenarios and possibilities that might have led to the unfortunate demise of Mr. Boullain. I will present our two strongest pieces of evidence."

"We have records of calls Mr. Ellington made to Mr. Boullain's home telephone and his cell phone number. He made back to back calls to Mr. Boullain."

Steele paced the front of the courtroom. He saw members of the Boullain family, their faces a mixture of grief and anger. Vengeance gleamed from Rick Boullain, Sr.'s eyes. Steele had seen such aggrieved expressions many times from victims' families who wanted justice for their loved one's death. But this was a preliminary trial, not a case trial. He knew from his boss's directive that the Boullain family expected victory, even if it wasn't the full-scale justice of a conviction.

Steele's eyes strayed to Tangi. He didn't want to look at her family, but he needed to convey that Devon Ellington was the prime suspect. It was legal strategy 101 to look the suspect in the eye—without hesitation. It communicated the prosecution's position that the person was guilty. Or, in this case, that he was the prime suspect.

But Steele had difficulty making eye contact with Devon Ellington. He had his own doubts about Devon's guilt. From the very beginning, he wasn't convinced that the two detectives had arrested the right person. And, most importantly, looking at Devon was like looking at Tangi. Seeing the an-

guish in her eyes speared his soul. If he'd known
that Devon was her brother he would have excused
himself from the case.

But he had to perform his professional responsibilities.

After presenting the lug reports from Rick Boullain's home and cell phone numbers, Steele called
the neighbor, Adam Hague, to the witness stand.
The neighbor repeated the information he'd
shared with the detectives. He was a credible, convincing witness . . . until defense attorney Ashton
Jeffries cross-examined him.

With a series of probing questions, Ashton was
able to show a very narrow timeline surrounding
Mr. Hague's testimony. And he presented other
possibilities concerning what could have occurred
on the night in question. One possibility included
testimony from another neighbor: Stanley Harris.

"You live across the street from Mr. Boullain,"
Ashton stated.

"My townhouse is directly across from his," said
Stanley Harris.

"Would you please share with us what you saw on
the night in question?"

"I saw a woman knocking on his door. She
knocked for a long time and then he opened the
door."

"Are you sure it was Rick Boullain?"

"Yes, I know him. We're courteous to each other."

"Continue."

"The woman had long blond hair and I could tell
she was attractive." Stanley stopped and gave the
judge an awkward smile. "I wish a woman like that

would visit me. Anyway, she hugged him when he opened the door and they were kissing."

"And you saw this from your window?"

Stanley nodded. "I probably shouldn't have been looking, but she was kissing him and let me tell you, he wasn't complaining."

"Could you please tell us what time you witnessed this?"

"It was after midnight."

"Thank you, sir," Ashton said, and returned to the defense table.

Steele listened to Stanley's testimony, angered that the detectives hadn't interviewed Stanley Harris. Since his townhouse was directly across the street from Rick's, he should have been immediately questioned. The detectives' ineptness had placed him in an awkward position. Even though the prosecuting timeline conflicted with this new evidence, his boss would still expect him to win. His only recourse was to attack the witness' character.

"Mr. Harris, are you lonely?" Steele asked.

Stanley's face turned red.

"Are you lonely?" Steele repeated.

Stanley looked at the judge. "What does that have to do with what I saw?"

"Please answer the question," directed Judge Whitaker.

"I'm not seeing anyone," he answered.

"When was the last time you had a date?"

"I don't know."

"One month, three months, six months ago?"

Stanley shrugged. "I don't remember the last time I had a date."

"So you're lonely."

"Yes, I'm lonely," Stanley shot back angrily. "But I still saw what I saw."

"Did you really? Why were you up at that time of night looking out the window?"

"Objection!" said Ashton.

"Your honor, I'm just trying to understand what kind of man Mr. Harris is, in order to determine how credible he is as a witness."

"I'll allow you a little leeway," said Judge Whitaker. "But make your point."

"Mr. Harris, please tell us why you were up late at night looking out the window?"

"I couldn't sleep."

"Do you frequently spy on your neighbors?"

"I wasn't spying."

"Are you a peeping Tom?"

"Objection!" shouted Ashton.

"Sustained," the judge said.

"Were you drinking that evening?"

"I had some wine."

"How much wine?"

"Maybe a glass."

"Are you sure it was one glass?"

"I had a glass with dinner, and then when I couldn't sleep I drank some more wine."

"How much more?"

Stanley shrugged. "I drank the rest of the bottle."

"So you drank a whole bottle of wine. Were you drunk when you were . . . peeping out the window?"

"I wasn't drunk," Stanley said defensively. "I wasn't peeping out the window."

"Since you spend a lot of time looking out the window, did you see Mr. Ellington when he arrived?"

"Yes."

"Did you see when he left?"

"No."

"You don't know when Mr. Ellington left?"

"No."

Steele stared at the witness for a minute. "That will be all."

"The witness may step down," Judge Whitaker said. Addressing the courtroom, he said, "We'll take a fifteen-minute break."

Steele successfully impeached the credibility of the defense's witness. During the fifteen-minute break, he found out that meek, nerdy-looking Stanley Harris was correct. The detectives had interviewed another witness who corroborated Stanley's testimony. A woman had visited Rick Boullain after Devon Ellington left the townhouse. The victim was seen opening the door to Isadora Graham, whom the detectives identified from telephone records. The detectives located the woman's place of residence, searched her apartment, and found a gun in the trash can in the back of her apartment building. Isadora Graham apparently had packed her suitcases and left the city. Both detectives were excited about finding a new suspect.

However, Robert Walsh did not want Steele to change his tactics in the courtroom.

"We can drop the charges later," Steele's boss said. "When we track this Isadora woman down and interview her, we'll drop the charges against Mr. Ellington. Hopefully she'll confess."

"What about the gun found near her apartment? If those bullets match, she's the prime suspect."

"That may be true, but it's too late to change our position. We have to play things out."

"This prelim is a farce. He's not a suspect," said Steele.

"He's still a suspect, and you need to treat this case as though he is."

"I disagree," said Steele. "I don't like playing with people's lives."

"Don't turn this into a racial issue," warned Robert.

"It's not about race," countered Steele. "Ellington's not a suspect, so we shouldn't pursue the charges any further."

"Nothing's changed. Right now we will continue to pursue charges against Mr. Ellington."

Steele checked his watch. "I need to get back in court."

"Steele, I'm ordering you to fully represent this office. I expect this case to be bound over for trial."

Twenty-two

"Your Honor," Steele said, rising from his chair. "It has come to our attention that some new evidence has been identified. This evidence requires further investigation and directly affects the proceedings today." Steele paused and cast a surreptitious glance at the defense table. "This evidence links the murder of Rick Boullain to another suspect. Therefore, we are dropping all charges against Devon Ellington. He is no—"

The rest of Steele's words were lost in a distorted symphony of sounds: joyful "ahs" and mournful "ohs," shouts of glee, and moans of grief. The loudest sounds came from the Ellington and Boullain families. Angry expressions glared on the faces of the Boullain family and amazed expressions adorned those of the Ellington family. Different remarks were made by the rest of the spectators in the courtroom, but spoken with the same tone—disbelief and shock.

"I wonder who really did it."

"Maybe they found the real killer."

"Maybe someone confessed."

"How dare they let him got off scot-free."

"Maybe he didn't do it."

"He must not have."

"I guess they shouldn't have charged him with murder before they had all the facts. That poor boy."

Devon released a long, shrill cry. "Thank you! Thank you! I'm free. Thank you!"

Everyone hovered around Devon—hugging him, kissing him, shaking his hand or slapping his back. Devon tried hard not to cry, but he couldn't hold back the tears. He wasn't the only who couldn't keep from crying. The only dry face belonged to Ashton Jeffries.

"Thank you, Mr. Jeffries, for saving my life," Devon said, hugging the older gentleman.

"You're welcome." Ashton patted Devon on the back. "My work is done. Now I shall have my afternoon tea."

"Let's go to lunch everybody," Tangi said, planting yet another kiss on Devon's cheek. "Name the place, Devon."

"I don't know." Devon wrinkled his brow for a moment. "Brielle's been itching to go to Moulin Rouge." He wrapped his arm around her waist. "How about there?"

"Wherever you want to go, whatever you want to do," Tangi exclaimed, her face bright with joy. "Just say it and we'll do it."

"I'm so glad this is over!" Devon gushed. "I'm so happy!"

"So are we," Romare said, wiping tears from his wife's face.

"Time to celebrate, celebrate," Devon sang, "And dance to the music."

"Not another oldies song!" Brielle exclaimed.

* * *

Before leaving the courtroom, Tangi eased over to the prosecutor's table. "Excuse me," she said, interrupting Steele's conversation with another district attorney.

"I'm Tangi Ellington," she said, her hand stretched outward.

Steele gently shook her hand, sending tiny waves of chills through both their bodies. "I'm Steele McDeal."

"Hello," Peter said to Tangi before walking away.

"So you're a model."

"And you're an attorney. A mean prosecuting attorney."

Steele searched her eyes trying to determine the depth of her anger. "I was doing my job." He dropped his voice to a whisper. "I didn't know."

Tangi studied his face, assessing the truth of his statement. Her heart knew the answer. She nodded, a soft smile on her lips. "Thank you. From the bottom of my heart, I thank you."

"The district attorney was fired!"

Who's the district attorney? Why should I care that he was fired? Tangi thought in the semi-consciousness of sleep. Slowly her mind filtered its way from mental inertia to the present moment. She wasn't in Bali on a video shoot, she was in her brother's guestroom. She hadn't dreamt that her brother was wrongly accused of murder. It really had happened.

"Wake up, Sleeping Beauty."

Gillian's voice sent her blasting back to reality.

"Who are you talking about?" She wiped her face with her hands. "Steele McDeal?"

"I didn't like him until he changed his tune yesterday." Gillian plopped on the edge of the bed. "I'm guessing that he knew that Devon was being unfairly charged."

Her head propped against the pillow, Tangi studied her sister-in-law's face. Strains from the last two weeks showed in the weariness on her face, but strength resonated in her gaze. It was there when Gillian's sister died shortly after meeting Romare. That steely strength was a source of attraction for Romare and a source of admiration for Tangi. She wondered if she had the courage to do what her heart was telling her.

"Why did they fire him?" Tangi asked.

"It was just on the news. The details were sketchy, but the reporter said he was fired for mishandling the preliminary trial related to the Rick Boullain murder." Gillian expelled a deep breath. "I guess he disagreed with his boss on how the case was being handled. I figured they must have found another suspect, but with today's news, he must have ruffled the wrong feathers when he dismissed the charges against Devon. Either that or he—"

"Didn't want to send my brother to prison."

Gillian crinkled her brows together.

"He knew how much my brother means to me."

Confusion washed over Gillian's face. "What are you talking about?"

"He didn't want to send my brother to prison." Tangi watched Gillian's face, waiting for her to understand the meaning of her words.

Comprehension showed in the form of her wide-opened mouth. "You know him?"

"He's John Doe," Tangi softly said.

"The man you met in Porta Plataea? The one who has you love struck?"

"I never said I was in love with him."

"You're still fighting it."

"I've never been in love before." She gave Gillian a thoughtful stare. "I don't know what I'm fighting."

"You didn't before, but you know now."

The meaning of Gillian's words sank in. Gillian was right. She'd felt it that last night in Porta Plataea and she felt it when she saw him in the elevator. The feeling had never disappeared. It kept growing inside of her, taking root inside her heart.

She fought her feelings, convincing herself there was a line between reality and fantasy. And when those worlds collided, it had an impact: a powerful explosion in their lives and an implosion in their hearts.

"Maybe I do," she said with a wistful smile. A sudden, devastating thought chased away that smile. "He probably hates me now. I cost him his job. He's been publicly embarrassed. He's not going to want to have anything to do with me."

"You don't know that for sure."

"Think about it, Gillian. If he'd sent Devon to prison, there'd be no way we could be together." She lapsed into introspection. "I told him about my family. He knew I wouldn't have anything to do with him."

"Maybe that's why he did it."

Tangi considered that possibility. "Maybe he did.

But I'm sure he didn't think he would lose his job over it." She paused for a moment. "He probably wishes I never walked into that courtroom."

The printer was slowly eking out a legal document with the words Request for Trial emblazoned on the page. Steele quickly glanced at the list of similar cases he'd found in Lexus-Nexis to verify that he had chosen the right cases for his father's lawsuit. The case was getting more and more intriguing each day. He was even able to identify similar cases that had been brought against other record companies. He learned that his father's record company, Egyptian Records, had willfully and intentionally misled his father. The court date was pending.

"You going to let them get away with firing you?" Jeremy placed a glass of iced tea on top of Steele's desk.

"I don't have any grounds, Pops."

"Make some up." Jeremy's eyes veered to the papers coming out of the printer.

"I knew what I was doing. I was ninety-nine percent sure that Walsh was going to fire me."

"Even with that new evidence?"

"I embarrassed the district attorney's office. I conducted myself in an insubordinate manner." Steele added more paper into the printer and pressed the flashing button. He faced his father. "The bottom line is this: he wanted me to pursue the case against Devon regardless of the evidence found."

"Even though they knew he didn't do it?" Still confused, Jeremy scratched his head. "And they were going to keep the charges against him until they found the person who did it?"

"That was the strategy."

Jeremy shook his head. "That's low."

"I've seen it happen a thousand times." Steele removed the papers from the printer. "I just couldn't let the brother go down like that."

"I think you did it because of her." Jeremy nodded at the picture of Tangi on the wall. "I don't blame you son," he said, chuckling.

"He wasn't guilty."

"I saw the way you stared at her picture that night I came here to talk with you about my lawsuit. I could see it in your eyes." Jeremy caught the direction of his son's gaze. "See, you're doing it now," he said, tapping Steele's shoulder. "When she walked into that courtroom you knew you'd never see her again if you convicted her brother."

"It wasn't that kind of trial."

"You know what I'm talking about. Now what I don't understand is how you fell in love with this woman when you didn't even know her real name."

"I didn't say I was in love with her."

Jeremy whisked his hand in a dismissive gesture, giving Steele an I-know-you're-in-love-with-her look. "How come you didn't know her name?"

"Pops, I can't really explain it. It wouldn't make sense to you."

"I was a celebrity for a little while. I might understand more than you think." He gave his son a thoughtful look. "Forget all that. I want to know what you plan on doing to get her into your life."

Twenty-three

Steele rang the doorbell, wondering what reaction his presence would bring. Standing outside the home of Romare and Gillian Ellington wasn't an entirely impulsive move. It was borne of thoughtful contemplation and morbid speculation. Even though he suspected that whomever opened the door wouldn't hesitate to slam the door in his face, he dared to stand there and find out.

His need to see Tangi had reached the boiling point. Steele tried to remain a respectful distance, giving the family time to recover from the crisis of Devon's arrest and hoping that the anger and hurt he'd caused Tangi had dissipated. He'd sent her an e-mail. It was a long e-mail, full of his thoughts and feelings. But she didn't respond. That wasn't his preferred choice of communication. He really wanted to hear her voice, see her face, hold her body. He had to find out if she felt the same for him as he did for her.

But, he didn't have her phone number.

"Hello, Mr. McDeal," Gillian said when she opened the door.

"Hello, Mrs. Ellington." A tentative smile was on his face. "May I come in?"

"Please do."

Steele studied her. Sincerity rang in her voice, and she didn't seem surprised or angered by his unannounced visit. "Thank you," he said, coming inside as she shut the door. "Let me formally introduce myself. I'm Steele McDeal."

"I'm Gillian Ellington. Tangi's sister-in-law." She paused for emphasis. "And you're John Doe."

The corner of his lips jerked with a tiny spasm. "She told you?"

A nod and soft smile was her answer.

Steele followed Gillian into the family room. She introduced him to Romare, Jordy, and Nolan.

"Let's go in the kitchen to talk," Romare said.

"I know this feels awkward," Steele said.

"Please have a seat." Romare gestured to the table.

Steele took a seat at the rectangular-shaped glass table surrounded by wrought iron chairs.

"Would you like something to drink or eat?" offered Gillian.

"No, thank you. First, I'd like to apologize for the anguish I've caused your family. From the beginning I thought the detectives were too hasty in their investigation, but once they had arrested Devon, my office was pressured to proceed."

"Did you think he was guilty?" Romare asked.

"No I didn't." A contemplative look came over his face. "The Boullain family is an interesting cast of characters and the detectives didn't do their job." He glanced at Gillian, then back at Romare. "When I saw him at the bond hearing, I didn't think he did it. I just sensed he wasn't that type of man. But my hands were tied."

Romare inclined his head. "We thank you for what you did at the preliminary trial. We're grateful you put an end to it."

"Devon is relieved and overjoyed," Gillian said. "He went on vacation with his girlfriend."

"I hope he has a great time." He paused for a moment. "How can I reach Tangi? Is she here?"

"Actually, she left this morning." Romare quietly assessed the man in his kitchen, the man who almost destroyed his brother's life. Had recent events not occurred, he might have had a friendlier disposition toward him. On the other hand, his position had softened when he found out that Steele had been involved with Tangi in Porta Plataea, which, he concluded, was the main reason he had dismissed the charges against Devon.

Romare still had difficulty understanding how they could have become so emotionally involved with each other without revealing themselves.

Disappointment was painfully evident on Steele's face. "I'd really like to get in touch with her." He spoke the words with urgency. "I need to talk to her."

"She thought you'd be upset because what you did for Devon cost you your job," Gillian said. "She didn't think you'd want to see her again."

Steele was completely shocked. "I knew it was going to happen. I defied my boss's order so I wasn't surprised when he fired me." He looked at Gillian and then Romare. "Besides, it really was the right thing to do."

An awkward silence followed.

"I have her e-mail address, but I'd really like to call her." Without thinking, he revealed the depth of his emotions when he said, "I want to hear her voice."

The longing in his voice was familiar to Gillian. She'd heard Tangi speak of him in the same way.

Steele watched the subtle exchange between husband and wife as Gillian looked at Romare before going over to the desk and retrieving a pen and paper. He wondered if they could hear his heart beating.

With a soft smile, Gillian handed Steele a piece of paper. "Here's Tangi's cell phone number and her home number in New York."

"Thank you, Mrs. Ellington." The sadness in his eyes disappeared, replaced by hope. Steele looked at Romare, and nodded in appreciation.

"Don't wait too long to call her," Gillian advised.

The penthouse suite at the exclusive Bali hotel was decorated to inspire romance. Everything was in place as if staged for a love scene in a movie or video—soft music playing, candles glowing, champagne flowing, the night breeze blowing.

When Tangi walked into Cricket's hotel room, there was no mistaking his expectations. The way he watched her during the video shoot communicated to everyone within sight that he wanted her. He didn't attempt to hide it. Tangi had to admit that she enjoyed being the object of his desire. She played the role, teasing and flirting with him. It was a diversion from the war raging inside her heart and mind. Her mind was winning: don't call Steele McDeal; he lost his job to save Devon.

Cricket's arms wrapped around her waist and their bodies began to move in a fluid motion to the sultry Caribbean-infused music. He whispered in her ear how much he wanted her and how he planned to make love to her. He promised that he wouldn't stop until she had had enough.

She hadn't been intimate with anyone since Steele, so she thought his whispered suggestions of his tongue exploring her secret garden would spark her passion. Yet, his promises of exquisite love-making didn't rouse her pulse.

She felt as cold inside as a winter ice storm.

Cricket felt the icy coolness of her response. "You're not feeling me, are you?" he asked, when the music stopped.

She raised her head and faced him with an honest expression on her face. She expected to see anger in his eyes, but instead there was only curiosity. "I don't know what to say. I don't want to offend you. You've been kind to me, generous and understanding, and—"

"You're not feeling my vibe."

"I know thousands of women would sleep with you, but I have somebody on my mind that . . . I can't seem to get out of my mind."

"I can make you forget him." His fingertips skimmed the soft curves of her face. "If only for one night."

"I know you could." She smiled wistfully, not doubting his sexual prowess. "I don't want to forget him."

Cricket accepted her decision with a slight nod.

"Thank you for everything." She sensed his disappointment. "No hard feelings, please?"

"You know you just bruised my ego. Shattered it to pieces. Now I'm going to have to see a therapist."

Tangi drew her brows together, unsure if he was serious or joking.

"It's cool, baby." He kissed her on the cheek. "I like a woman who knows her heart."

Tangi returned to her hotel room. She changed into a pencil-strap silk nightgown. Beckoned by the balmy night breeze, she went out onto the balcony, her cell phone in hand. An unfamiliar number appeared in the caller ID display. It was a New Orleans number. Assuming it was a call about her family, she hit the return-call button without listening to her messages.

The voice that answered melted her heart. "Hello."

"Steele?"

"Tangi?"

"I didn't know it was your number."

"Am I too late?" he asked.

"Too late for what?"

"I went to your brother's house to get your number. By the way, they are wonderful people. I remembered the way you described them. When I met them, I knew why you had said the things you did." He paused for a moment. "Considering the circumstances, they were very gracious, which made it easier for me to ask for your number."

"I didn't think you'd want to see me."

"I dropped the charges against your brother because there was no case against him."

"And you lost your job over it."

"I was flooded with offers the next day. But, I decided to join a small law firm."

"I'm glad. I felt really guilty."

"I also did it because of you."

"I know."

They were silent for a long moment.

"So am I too late?" he asked again.

"I don't know what you mean."

"Gillian suggested that I shouldn't wait long before contacting you. I didn't think too much of it when she said it, but driving away I wondered if you were going to get married or—"

"No, that wasn't it."

"Tell me."

Tangi pondered her words before answering. "She knew I was being pursued by someone who really wanted me."

"So am I too late?" he repeated, hoping she hadn't given her heart or body to another.

"I didn't want him the same way he wanted me."

"Tangi, I want to see your face. I want to see you smile. I want to make you happy. I want to hear your crazy laugh."

She giggled, his words like music to her soul.

"I want to touch you," he continued.

"What would you do?"

"I would hold you tight, caress your body right, then whisper, 'Don't move.'"

Tangi closed her eyes as a powerful memory overtook her senses, taking her back to that moment in time when he first made love to her. She realized what was so different that night: she felt complete.

"I would tell you that I love you."

"And I love you," she whispered.

Twenty-four

The night before Steele's arrival was the longest night of Tangi's life. At her New York penthouse apartment, she had tried sleeping, but all she'd been able to do was lie in her canopy bed, her mind full of memories of Porta Plataea. She had tried reading, watching a movie, listening to music. But nothing distracted her. No amount of escapist entertainment could distract her thoughts from Steele.

At 3:00 in the morning she'd considered calling him, just to reassure herself that his plans hadn't changed. She dialed his number but hung up before it rang. She had thought missing him had made her crazy, but anticipating his arrival was almost as nerve-racking. Almost.

With excruciating slowness, the endless night had stretched into morning and daylight revealed rays of sunshine behind a spattering of clouds.

High above Fifth Avenue, Tangi awoke with the feeling that she hadn't slept at all. She probably had had less than two hours of sleep. But it didn't matter—Steele would be arriving soon. Sitting bolt upright, she stretched luxuriously. After such a restless night, she should have felt groggy and grumpy, but instead she was full of joyful anticipation.

Tangi flung aside the covers and popped out of
bed. Humming cheerfully to herself, she slipped
into a teal silk robe trimmed with ostrich feathers
and wiggled her feet into fuzzy teal slippers. It was
time to get dressed.

Hearing the airplane's wheels hit the runway at
John F. Kennedy Airport, Steele's heart began to
race. He wasn't one of those travelers who's afraid
of take-offs and landings. His heart raced in anticipation of seeing Tangi Ellington. Not mysterious
Jane, but Tangi Ellington.

He missed her.

He wanted to hold her.

He wanted to kiss her lips.

He wanted to see her eyes when he confessed his
love to her.

And soon, he would.

Steele took a taxi from the airport to Tangi's up-
scale Fifth Avenue address. Now that he knew who
she really was, he was even more mystified by her. It
was as if he were assembling a puzzle, snapping together a few pieces, but far from completing the
puzzle.

The taxi driver attempted to make conversation
with Steele, but he soon realized that Steele wasn't
a talkative passenger. Even though he'd had a
three-hour plane ride to contemplate things, Steele
was still too busy thinking about Tangi to hold a
trivial conversation with the taxi driver, whose thick
accent was difficult to understand.

Remembering the conversation with his mother
and sister, he couldn't help smiling, even though

he knew he'd been the butt of their joke. They profusely teased him about not recognizing Tangi. They were perplexed that he really didn't know who she was. Camille pointed at the picture he'd painted and bluntly asked, "How come you didn't know that was her?"

Steele had shrugged. "I don't pay much attention to celebrities."

Jana grabbed some magazines with Tangi on the cover from Steele's coffee table. "How the hell did you not know that was her?"

"I told you: I don't pay attention to celebrities. I might recognize someone's face but I don't know their name."

In his heart of hearts, he knew that he'd somehow intentionally put himself in a state of ignorance. He knew that she had more at stake by revealing herself. Besides, Porta Plataea's claim to fame was protecting its guests' identity. Most of its guests were rich and famous.

He deliberately didn't let his mind probe the reasons why she didn't want to reveal her true name. They were on vacation, miles away from their real lives and they were enjoying themselves. Did who they were really matter? He'd convinced himself that it didn't. The we-don't-need-to-know-who-we-really-are game was over when they left the island.

But it really did matter. It mattered because the game wasn't over. Their hearts were in control. Their hearts were rewriting the rules of the game.

At the sound of the doorbell, Tangi's heart raced like a speeding train. The waiting was finally over.

Steele McDeal, not John, was on the other side of her door.

She surveyed her reflection in the mirror. She was dressed in red, white, and black—A flaring, red satin mini-skirt, a silky white blouse, and black pantyhose and heels. Tangi ran her fingers through her loose black curls and squirted French perfume on her arms, wrists, and the back of her neck. She was ready.

"Just a minute," she said when the doorbell rang again. She swung the door open wide, but upon seeing him, her heart opened even wider.

"Good afternoon," Steele said, holding a bouquet of roses in his hand.

"Good afternoon."

A long moment passed. She had no idea how long they stood there, absorbing each other's presence. She felt like a teenager again—all arms and legs and no tongue. They stared at each other, like two lost puppies that had found their way home.

"These are for you," he said, handing her the roses.

"Thank you." Being near him she could feel a rush of warmth reaching out to her. It was as if a flurry of sparks had burst inside her and was swiveling all through her body. "Come in," she finally said.

Steele followed her into the living room. "So this is how the rich and famous live," he blithely commented.

She whipped her head around, unsure of his meaning. Upon seeing the merriment in his eyes, she said. "That's why I didn't tell you."

"I know." His tone was full of understanding and sincerity.

"And I didn't think what happened . . . would have happened."

"Neither did I," he said, sitting down on the sofa beside her.

They held each other's gaze. The atmosphere was supercharged with so much sexual energy that she half-expected to see electrical currents ricocheting throughout her apartment.

"I'm really curious about something. Did you really not know who I am?"

"No, I didn't." He looked at her intently. "My mother and sister have relentlessly teased me. When Jana saw the painting, she said you looked very familiar, but she couldn't place your name with your face."

"My family thought I was crazy. Romare shook his head and said, 'You've gone totally Hollywood.'"

"You gave no clues about yourself. I didn't know your last name or where you were born." He grew quiet a minute. "If I had any idea that Devon Ellington was your brother, I would have handled the situation differently. I wouldn't have been able to stop the arrest, but I'm very sorry for the pain that I caused your family."

She gave him a thoughtful stare, reflecting on the conversation she had had with her family about Steele. Gillian sensed the emotional conflict and even Devon—who'd suffered the most—was forgiving. Neither blamed Steele, nor were they bitter. Romare was a bit more reticent about her relationship with Steele. He had a hard time believing that Steele didn't know who she was. "He could have looked on the Internet and found out that you grew up in New Orleans and have two brothers," Romare had remarked.

"I never told him who I was and he didn't recognize me," she'd explained.

"It doesn't seem possible," Romare had said.

"It happened. The fact that we didn't know our true identities is why our feelings went wild."

In the end, Romare had said, "If Devon doesn't have a problem with it, I don't have a problem with it. If you feel that strongly about him, I would never stand in the way of your happiness."

Tangi's thoughts returned to the moment at hand. Looking at Steele, she felt that love was finally within her reach. She wanted to grab hold of it and never let it go. "Apology accepted."

"Does your family think you're crazy for seeing me?"

"Before everything happened with Devon, Gillian was encouraging me to call you. And Devon is so easygoing. He's just relieved that it's over and deep down he's mourning the death of his friend. He and Rick were friends."

"I never thought about that."

"But Romare is skeptical."

"I sensed it."

"He'll accept my decision. Ultimately, they know you did the right thing by Devon. And you did it for the right reasons."

"I've seen too many brothers railroaded by the system." He reached over and grabbed her hand. "I've missed you so much." He leaned toward her, and lifting her chin, brushed a gentle kiss across her pliant lips.

"I've thought about you every day. I would go to sleep thinking about you and wake up thinking about you," she said. "I thought about calling you. Sometimes I picked up the phone and dialed your number, but then hung up before it even rang."

"Why didn't you call?"

"Because I was afraid," she said in a husky whisper.

"Afraid of what?"

She pondered his question. Her face underwent a subtle change, as though a shadow had slipped under her skin. A shadow that challenged her to be honest. Eyes closed, she let out a soft sigh. "Afraid of this moment," she finally said. "Afraid of finding out that you really are just my fantasy man."

He kissed her fingertips, his eyes reaching out and drowning in hers. "Are you afraid now?"

"Not anymore." She stared at him through thoughtful eyes. "In that courtroom, of all places, I was fascinated by you. Just watching you work, I wanted to know so much more about you. You became a real man."

"How ironic." He compressed his lips for a moment. "You became even more of a fantasy. I did a search on the Internet about you. You're a supermodel." He stopped and laughed. "I discovered why you have that sexy walk."

A trace of a smile appeared on her lips. "It took a lot of practice."

"You're famous." His eyes roamed around the room. "You're a wealthy young woman."

"But underneath it all . . . I'm real."

"That's why I'm here. Because even after I found out your real name, I remembered the woman from the island. I had already met the essence of who you really are."

"My essence," she said with a giggle.

"I'm amazed by your devotion to your family." He smiled at her. "You even recently met my mother."

"When?"

"When you visited your sister-in-law's mother."

"Mama Ruby?"

"My mother's a nurse and Gillian's mother was her patient. She said you were real nice to everyone and turned Miss Ruby's room into a veritable garden."

"I remember her. Camille," she said, smiling fondly. "Mama Ruby said she was the only nurse that she liked."

"Isn't that an interesting coincidence?"

"Very interesting," she said, staring into his face, just inches from hers. Suddenly, her heart was beating erratically.

Steele returned her stare, and an unexpected wave of heat engulfed him.

The moment seemed to stretch into eternity.

She was acutely aware of his long, lean-muscled physique, the cleft in his chin, and his lips, which seemed to have one purpose—kissing.

He was acutely aware of her beautiful brown skin and the curve of her lips.

The moment ended with a kiss—a long kiss that ended in Tangi's bedroom, prompting a series of kisses and an endless lovemaking session.

Ruby pursed her lips together, her eyes surveying the street just two blocks away from her house as

Gillian steered the Lincoln Navigator closer to their destination. "Everything looks the same."

"You haven't been gone that long," Gillian said, casting her mother a sideways glance.

"I ain't been gone this long before," Ruby said. "Not in thirty-three years."

"You've lived here for thirty-three years?" Jordy asked, sitting in the driver's side back seat.

"We moved into this house before Mikey was born."

"That's a long time, Grandma."

"A long time," repeated Nolan.

Gillian noticed Aunt Mary's car parked a block away from her mother's house. Suspecting that her aunts were planning a surprise party, she sped past the old black Cadillac, hoping her mother didn't notice the car.

"Beatrice finally painted her house," Ruby said, pointing to the yellow one-story house. "And she painted her fence yellow. That's too much yellow for me."

"I like yellow," said Nolan. "That's my favorite color."

"I thought blue was your favorite color," said Jordy.

"It's yellow."

"And tomorrow it might be green," Gillian said, giving her son a quick smile.

"I like green, Mommy."

Jordy laughed. "You're a silly boy."

"I'm a silly boy."

"We're here," Gillian announced, parking in front of her mother's house.

"Look at my house." Her hand draped across her chest, she said, "My heart is beating so fast."

Jordy lurched forward. "Grandma, you okay?"

"Sugar, Grandma is just fine. My heart is beating with joy."

"Oh," Jordy gushed with relief.

"I'm happy to be home." Turning back to view her home, Ruby said, "I didn't think I'd ever see home again."

"Let's go inside," Gillian said.

"Yeah! We're going into Grandma's house," Nolan cried.

"Jordy, help Nolan out of his car seat and I'll help Grandma."

"Okay," Jordy said.

"I can get out by myself." Nolan released the buckle and jumped out of the seat.

By the time Gillian went around to open the passenger door, Ruby had already opened the door and was stepping out of the car. "Let me help you, Mama."

"I'm fine, honey." She eased over to the front porch. "Aw, look at the pretty flowers."

"Mikey planted them for you," Gillian said.

"They're beautiful."

Leaning on the railing, Ruby slowly climbed up the three steps to her front porch, which held two rocking chairs and a glider. She reached the front door, and before she could turn the doorknob, the door swung open.

"Surprise!" shouted her two sisters, Mary and Lizzie.

"Don't give me a heart attack."

"Mama, don't say that," chided Gillian.

At last, Ruby was at home. She saw the WELCOME HOME sign spread across the doorway to the living room. "I'm not surprised. I saw your car down the street."

"Mama, I didn't think you saw it!" exclaimed Gillian. "I went fast so you wouldn't see it."

"You should have come from the other direction," Ruby chided.

"I didn't know." Gillian patted Aunt Mary's shoulder. "But I'm not surprised."

"Look at the balloons, Mommy," Nolan said, reaching for one. "Can I have one?"

"Of course, baby." Aunt Mary removed a red balloon from the archway and gave it to Nolan, along with a big, sloppy kiss.

"Thank you," Nolan beamed.

"Let me sit down for a spell," Ruby said, easing down on her slip-covered sofa. Ruth's modest living room was decorated with framed photographs that chronicled the growth of her family.

"You okay?" Aunt Mary asked.

"I'm fine. I was at the hospital for three weeks and then Gillian kidnapped me for two weeks."

"Grandma, we didn't kidnap you," Jordy said, giggling. "We took care of you."

"I know, baby. You took good care of me. I appreciate it." She chuckled. "You're good kidnappers."

Jordy laughed. "Grandma!"

"Grandma!" mimicked Nolan.

"I'm just glad to be here," Ruby said. "There's no place like home."

"Grandma, that's my line in *The Wizard of Oz*." Jordy clicked her heels together, and closed her eyes, repeating the words, "There's no place like home. There's no place like home. There's no place like home." Opening her eyes, she smiled when they all clapped.

"I can't wait to see you in your play," Aunt Lizzie said.

"There's no place like home," Nolan said.

"Dorothy was right," Ruby said.

Twenty-five

The movie preview party was in full swing, the sea of rising voices drowning out the strains of the musical ensemble. Everyone seemed to know one another. Laughter, whispers, catty remarks, and secrets were exchanged between sips of expensive champagne.

Steele surveyed the scene, amazed by the transformation of the New York hotel to reflect the movie's avante garde art theme. It was a kaleidoscope of mesmerizing colors and intermingling textures. Art was everywhere: in the atmosphere, in the decorations, in the eclectic music played by the new age band, and in the clothes that adorned the stylish guests.

Steele had attended many formal parties and social gatherings in New Orleans, but this was very different. Tangi had warned him: "Expect the unexpected."

Climbing the red-carpeted stairs, their arrival was announced by the master of ceremonies. The media ascended upon them with cameras and microphones. Waiting in the background, he watched as Tangi granted interviews, smiling and talking to reporters from different media outlets.

Red-carpet interviews finished, they entered the

resplendent lobby with its grand staircase. Tangi circulated the room, introducing Steele as she engaged in brief conversations before moving to the next person or group of people. Along the way, Tangi and Steele were separated.

Several hours later, back at her penthouse apartment, Steele quietly unzipped Tangi's rhinestone-encrusted, column-shaped gown. She stepped out of the gown and hung it in her room-sized closet. Wearing a strapless bra and thong, she sat down at the dressing table.

"Now I know how Stedman probably feels."

A sinking sensation descended upon her. He'd been unusually quiet in the limo, making casual remarks about the movie—"I don't think it will be a box-office hit"—and the sarcastic comments about the preview party—"It was over the top, but it seems everything in your world is over the top."

He'd accompanied her to other events and they invariably were always separated. Steele would either be standing alone or engaged in conversation while waiting for her. Whenever they reconnected, he'd greet her with a warm smile. But this evening, the smile was patently fake, a mask to please the cameras.

"What does that mean?" she asked, viewing herself in the mirror. She knew this moment would come, the moment when he'd decide that their lives were too different. Three months into their love affair, spending every weekend together, Steele was going to end the relationship.

"Sometimes I feel . . . uncomfortable. Media attention is more than a notion. I understand now why some celebrities cry foul."

"I know," she softly said.

"But I'm not in the spotlight." He stood behind her, their eyes meeting in the dressing table mirror. "You are."

"Can you handle it?"

"At times I feel like a fish out of water. There are awkward moments when it's obvious that I don't belong. But that's okay. I don't let it bother me."

"I guess I'd feel like a fish out of water in a courtroom."

"Exactly." Steele ran his fingers across her neckline. "Your world has a bigger, broader scope, but I'm adjusting."

"I'm glad," she said, smiling with relief. "I thought you were going to . . . bolt."

"Bolt?"

"But in a nice way. I thought you were going to say, 'I can't deal. This is too much. Our worlds are too different.'"

"I'm secure about who I am. I'm proud of your success, but I'm happy that you are you," he said with tender emotion. "I fell in love with you, not the media personification of you." He bent over and kissed her mouth.

"I love you, too," Tangi said. "I'm very glad that you're not star-struck or overwhelmed by it all. This life—this madness—can spin your head around and make you forget who you are. I've seen it happen too many times."

"When we're out somewhere and we get separated or the media acts like I don't exist—"

"Don't say that—"

"They do. That's the truth of the matter. But it doesn't matter to me. All I'm thinking is: I'm the one who gets to go home with her; I'm the one who gets to do this . . . " Steele softly nibbled on her neck. "And I get to do this." He unhooked her bra. "I'm the one who makes love to you."

Steele's dismissal from the New Orleans Parish District Attorney's office was reported in the local news and frequently mentioned when there were stories about the murder of Rick Boullain. It was a story that generated frequent media coverage.

So when Isadora Graham was charged and arrested for Rick's murder some six months later, various members of the media contacted Steele for his opinion on the news-breaking events. They arrived at his new law firm—Fitzpatrick, Burke and McDeal—without an appointment.

But Steele declined the opportunity of an on-camera interview. Determined to get a quote from Steele, a rather ambitious, young female reporter cornered him in the men's bathroom.

"Here's your chance to let the world know that you were right when you dropped the charges against Devon Ellington," the reporter said, appearing from a bathroom stall while Steele was washing his hands. "You've been vindicated. I know you have something to say."

"No comment," he said with a wry smile.

"She confessed to murdering Rick Boullain and even admitted to sleeping with Rick *and* his father," the reporter said, incredulity in her tone. "Did you know that?"

"No comment."

"Do you refuse to comment because of your involvement with Tangi Ellington, sister to Devon Ellington?" probed the reporter. "Is that the real reason why you dropped the charges?"

Steele met the reporter's intense gaze. "No comment."

"It wouldn't matter now anyway."

Steele dried his hands with a paper towel, and then tossed it into the trash. "No comment." Steele opened the door to leave, but stopped midway. "I will admit to something."

The reporter positioned her pen to take notes on the small pad. "Yes," she said, expectantly.

"I admire your determination to get the story."

She gave him a small smile and shrugged her shoulders.

When Steele returned to his office, he found an envelope on his desk chair. The outside of the envelope was blank. He opened it and found a sheet of a paper with the words—Morelli Never Forgets—printed in boldface type.

Steele remembered the words Morelli mouthed at his trial: You're a dead man.

Wondering who'd been in his office, Steele questioned his secretary. "Did you see anyone come into my office?"

"No," she said. "With all the media madness, there've been all kinds of people in here."

"We need to tighten security," he said, and then returned to his desk. Steele picked up the telephone and dialed his former associate Peter Schwartz.

"Hello, Peter. It's Steele."

"Steele, I can't believe you're not making comments about the Boullain murder. If you were still here, Robert would be forced to admit that he was wrong."

"It's old news to me. Listen, I'm calling because I've just been threatened by Morelli."

"How so?"

"Someone left me a note with the words: Morelli Never Forgets."

"Sounds ominous."

"That's why I'm calling. I'm going to send the envelope and note over for you to check for prints and any clues."

"Consider it done."

"See if you can find out who Morelli's been in touch with in jail. His attorney claimed that he had some contacts with the Patterson crime syndicate that the feds are investigating."

"It's going to be a major shakedown. Major RICO charges," said Peter. "You know I have a friend in the FBI."

"Let me know what you find out," said Steele.

"I will," Peter said, before steering the conversation into personal terrain. "What's it like dating a celebrity?"

Steele pondered the question; this wasn't the first time the question had been asked. "I don't know how to answer that. We're making it work; that's all I can say."

"I heard you're really serious about Ms. Tangi Ellington."

"You heard right," Steele said.

"I'm happy for you. I'll be in touch."

"Thanks, Peter."

"No problem. Just be careful."

Twenty-six

All eyes were on Jordy. In a blue gingham cotton dress and ruby red slippers, she stood in the center of the stage and closed her eyes. She clicked her heels together and softly repeated, "There's no place like home. There's no place like home. There's no place like home."

The stage lights turned dark for several moments. When the lights came up, Dorothy was in a different place. She was at home in her bed, surrounded by her family.

As the audience watched the final scene, tears dotted the eyes of family and friends watching the middle school theatrical production of *The Wizard of Oz*.

Everyone stood and clapped fervently when the cast members took their bows. The audience's cheers grew louder and louder until it reached a crescendo when Jordy took her final bow.

Ruby, Gillian, Romare, Nolan, Devon, Brielle, Tangi and Steele—sitting in the front row—rose from their chairs and each presented Jordy with a single red rose. Swarmed by a sea of faces, Jordy heard an array of compliments.

"You can really sing, girl."

"You need to get that child an agent."

"'Somewhere Over the Rainbow' is my favorite song. You sang it perfectly."

"She got talent, all right. One day, she gonna be a superstar."

"Just like her Auntie Tangi."

Eyes shining with pride and joy, Jordy graciously expressed gratitude for their support and love. Sterling and her half-brothers gave her a group hug.

Tangi kissed Jordy's cheek and warmly embraced her. "You got skills," she teased.

"Thank you."

"I'm serious. Let me know if you want to take this further because I can—"

"Not just yet," Gillian said. "I think Jordy needs to have a normal—"

"Childhood," said Jordy.

"If that doesn't sound like something Romare would say," remarked Tangi.

"Maybe it is," Gillian said, shrugging. "It just so happens that I think the same way. She should just be a kid. She has plenty of time."

Tangi tucked her hand under Jordy's chin. "What do you think?"

"I'm not one hundred percent sure I want to be an actress. I'd kind of like to be a lawyer." She grinned at Tangi and Gillian. "Maybe I could be the first woman president."

"You go, girl," Tangi said. "Dream big."

"Auntie Gigi, what did I say?" A puzzled expression was on Jordy's face. "Why are you all teary-eyed?"

"That's something your mother would say."

Gillian dabbed away her tears and tightly hugged Jordy. "She would be so proud of you."

"I hate to interrupt this . . . cry fest," said Steele, "but they want take pictures of the cast."

"Okay," Jordy said.

"I know everyone has commended you on your performance, but I haven't." He grinned at her. "You were outstanding, Miss Jordy Peyton."

"Thank you, Mr. Steele," she said, before walking away.

"And I thought the women in *my* family were emotional," Steele said. "Crying over a middle school play."

"Don't tell me you weren't moved?" challenged Tangi.

"Not to tears. Movies and plays don't make me cry."

"So, something very bad has to happen."

He gave her a thoughtful look. "Like if there was no me and you," he said tenderly.

Gazing into his eyes, she could feel her heart beating. "Are you trying to make me cry?"

He pulled her into his embrace and kissed her on the forehead. "I'd rather fill your heart with love."

"And you can have all my love."

Steele kissed Tangi on the forehead, and whispered into her ear: "Can't wait till I get you in bed."

Nolan suddenly said, "Mommy, Mr. Steele is kissing Auntie Tangi again."

It was 5:45 P.M. when Steele's office telephone rang. It was the end of the day and he didn't want to be distracted from the case he was working on, so he didn't answer. Five minutes later, the phone rang again.

It rang four times before he finally answered. "Hello."

"Steele, I'm glad I caught you."

"Hey, Peter. What's going on?"

"You're okay, right?"

"Yeah, what's up?"

"You were right about Morelli."

"What are you talking about?"

"Morelli's coming after you. He put a hit on you."

"How do you know this?"

"The person he used to hire the killer is in custody trying to make a deal. He told us he acted as a go-between for Morelli," Peter explained. "By the way, when is your birthday?"

"Today."

"Today?"

"Yes, today. What's so significant about my birthday?"

"Today is the day the hit is supposed to happen."

"What?" Steele reached inside the desk drawer for his gun.

"I don't know how or when or where. I just know it's supposed to take place on your birthday."

Steele swallowed. "I shouldn't be surprised, but I am."

"I'll send some officers over there right away. They'll go home with you and stay with you until the hit man is arrested."

"Tangi's there!" Fear ripped through his veins.

"Oh shit! I'll send some officers to your place right now."

"Don't worry about me. Make sure Tangi's safe."

Steele hung up from Peter and immediately called Tangi's cell phone.

"Happy birthday, honey," she said, upon answering. "I have a big surprise for you."

"Tangi, please listen to me carefully. Make sure all the windows and doors are locked."

"What . . . what are you talking about?"

"Try not to panic. Are you standing near a window?"

"Yes."

"Go into the bathroom. But first make sure the doors are locked."

"Steele, you're scaring me. What's going on?"

"Are you checking the doors?"

"Yes," she said in an edgy tone.

"I don't want to frighten you, but some police officers are on their way. Don't let anyone in except the police."

"Steele, what the hell is going on?"

"I just got a call from Peter from the DA's office. A man I convicted of murder and sent to prison has hired someone to kill me."

"Oh no!" Her stomach knotted in fear for herself and Steele.

"Luckily, Peter found out about it."

"Does he know when? Where? How?"

"He knows it's supposed to happen today!"

"Oh no," she muttered.

"Peter also knows who the person is. The police are looking for him now. In the meantime, they're on the way there. Please don't go anywhere."

She locked herself inside the bathroom. "I'm scared, Steele. I feel like a sitting duck."

"I'm sorry, baby. Whoever it is might be lurking outside. I think you're safer inside."

"Okay."

"I'm leaving now. The police should be there in five or ten minutes."

"Okay," she sobbed.

"If I was there I'd wipe your tears away and I—"

"Steele, I heard something. It sounded like a gun shot."

"Tangi, be careful. I love you."

"I love you, too. Hurry, Steele, hurry!" Her cell phone emitted a high-pitched tone. She read the message on her cell phone: signal lost.

Epilogue

Cameras flashed at Tangi and Steele, capturing the stylishly-dressed couple exiting arm-in-arm from the premiere showing of VH5's *People and Places of Style* hosted by Tangi Ellington. Smiling, they posed for the media before getting into a black stretch limousine.

"I'm really starting to enjoy this lifestyle," Steele said as the limousine drove away from Radio City Music Hall.

"What, no more I hate celebrities stuff? No more they're selfish, arrogant, rude—"

"How can I complain? I fell in love with one."

Their gazes held for a moment, then she smiled. "And I fell in love with a mean prosecuting attorney who tried to put my brother in jail."

"I'm very sorry about that unfortunate incident at my apartment," he said.

"I know," she said, reflecting on the frightening five minutes when she was locked in his bathroom, listening to a barrage of gunfire. It was the longest five minutes of her life, ending with the police bursting into the apartment. Tangi had refused to come out of the bathroom until she heard Steele's voice. "I don't like thinking about it. It's over and I hope nothing like that happens again." Emphatically, she added, "Ever. I'm glad you moved."

"I had to."

They were quiet for a while.

"I was so proud of you tonight," he finally said. "They picked the right person when they chose you to be the host." The premiere showing of the video network's new show drew top designers and style-setters in the fashion and music industries. All types of celebrities attended the event dressed in outfits suitable for the Academy Awards.

"Are you just saying that?

"I'm serious, baby. You bring credibility to the show. You give new meaning to the saying, 'beauty and brains.'"

She couldn't stop the smile from forming on her lips. "Thank you." His compliment meant more to her than the rave reviews from critics and fans.

Steele opened the bar compartment and grinned when he saw the opened bottle of champagne. He poured champagne into two glasses.

"It was Cricket who was pursuing you when I called you in Bali? The one that you didn't want as much as he wanted you?"

She bobbed her head. "How do you know?"

"The way he looked at you. I saw it in his eyes."

"Cricket changed the video production schedule and flew me back to the states when I found out about Devon. He tried to romance me, and when I turned him down, he didn't get angry. He didn't flip on me."

Steele handed her a glass of champagne. "With his ego?"

"I was surprised, too. But he's cool. His clothing

line is going to be featured in one of our segments." She sipped some champagne. "You kept me in suspense long enough. What happened in court today?"

"Are you questioning my ability to win? Are you questioning my legal skills? Are you—"

"No," she giggled. "I just want confirmation. I figured you were holding out because of the amount."

"We won big time. Egyptian Records owes my father a half-million dollars."

"Congratulations!" She planted affectionate kisses on his cheek.

"Now he can live like a celebrity. And I'm now representing two other singers who had slave contracts with record companies."

"So you really don't mind this . . . lifestyle? Traveling back and forth from New York to New Orleans, traveling to my assignments."

Tangi and Steele lived in separate cities, but they usually spent weekends together. They talked several times a day, and never went to bed without saying good night to each other. Video conferencing cameras were installed in both their homes, so they could see each other even when they were miles and miles apart.

"It's an unordinary life," Tangi said.

"We have an unordinary love."

"An unordinary love, indeed," she said, caressing his face and running her fingers across his lips.

Steele pressed the intercom button and directed the limo driver not to disturb them. Sliding closer together, and then moving as one, their mouths came together in a passionate kiss. His hand slid up her throat and curled around the base of her neck.

Their lips never left each other while their hands struggled to remove clothing.

Steele pulled down the straps on her evening gown, the sight of her breasts drawing him like bees to honey. He had to taste them: he kissed the full curve, then the dark center. His tongue flicked roughly, hungrily, lustfully.

"Steele," she groaned as sensations swirled from her breast throughout the rest of her body.

Steele unzipped his pants and freed himself from his trousers. Her fingers encircled the rigid length of his penis and then she caressed its velvety tip with the ball of her thumb.

"I want you now," he said, sliding on a condom before stretching her back against the length of the limo seat.

She pulled the length of her evening gown upward while Steele lowered her panties. Positioning himself above her, their mouths met for another deep, wet kiss. He spread her legs, then guided his erection into the softness between her legs, nestled in the vee of dark curls.

Inside her velvety smoothness, he moved slowly and deeply. "This is going to be a long and slow ride," he whispered into her ear. "Don't move."

Head tilted back, eyes closed, legs stretched open, pleasure seeping from every part of her body, she moaned, "I'm not going anywhere."

"Lookie, lookie, there's Auntie Tangi," Nolan said, pointing at the big screen television showing the premiere of VH5's *People and Places of Style*. Nolan ran to the screen and pointed to the image of Tangi interviewing a well-known fashion designer.

Sitting on the sofa in the theatre room on the bottom level of his home, Romare said, "We see her, son."

"Move out of the way," Jordy said.

"Okay, okay," Nolan said, running over and bouncing on top of Romare's lap.

"You're getting so big." Tangi gently rubbed Gillian's protruding belly.

"Don't you know she's got a baby in there?" Nolan asked.

"I thought there was a watermelon in there." Tangi kissed the top of Nolan's head.

Nolan rubbed his mother's belly. "Mommy said I was in her tummy, but I don't remember being in there."

Everyone in the room—Tangi, Steele, Romare, Gillian, Devon, Brielle, and Jordy—laughed.

"Aw, it's over," Jordy said when credits rolled on the projection screen.

"Great job Tangi," said Romare.

Jordy gave her aunt a big hug. "You're my super role model."

"It's going to be a hit show," Devon predicted.

"Definitely," agreed Brielle.

"Thank you, thank you," Tangi said. "Sometimes I have to fight with the producers to maintain the quality, but I'm proud of the show."

"Listen up," Gillian said, rubbing her belly. "I have an announcement to make."

Conversations stopped, and all eyes were on Gillian, waiting for her to speak. The announcement however, came from Romare. "We're having twins."

"So that's why you're so big," Tangi said.

Brielle hugged Gillian. "Congratulations."

"Twins?" Devon looked bewildered. "I didn't know twins ran in our family."

Tangi shrugged nonchallantlly. "I don't think it does."

"What are you trying to say?" teased Gillian. "Romare's not the baby's daddy?"

"I meant—"

"For your information, my dear brother-in-law, the twin gene comes from my side of the family. My grandfather was a twin."

"So I better not get it twisted," quipped Devon.

"Exactly."

"You're not the only one with big news," Devon said, grabbing Brielle's hand and drawing her into his arms. "Brielle and I are going to—"

"Get married!" Jordy screamed, jumping up and down.

Devon and Brielle both became quiet. Embarrassed expressions claimed their faces. An awkward silence passed. Finally, Devon said, "Yes, we are!"

"You were trying to trick us," said Jordy.

"Just joking with you, shorty," Devon teased.

"Congratulations," Gillian said, hugging Brielle. "Have you set a date?"

"Not yet. We're still shopping for a ring," Brielle said.

"We're very busy at work. We just signed a new client the other day," Devon said. "Brielle keeps the business in check."

"Popcorn's almost ready," Romare announced, standing behind the bar near the free-standing air popcorn machine. Everyone gathered around the bar area, getting bowls for the popcorn and glasses for drinks.

"Congratulations, man," Steele said to Devon.

"She stuck by me through thick and thin," Devon said, observing Brielle helping Nolan get a bowl. "Most girls would have booked when I got arrested."

"I'm grateful that you're not holding a grudge against me. If you did, I wouldn't be standing here right now."

"The bottom line is you set me free. So I don't have any beef with you." Devon picked up the television remote and turned the volume down. "I can't believe they're having a trial almost a year later. Isadora confesses to killing Rick. She had an affair with Rick and his father, then kills Rick because he wouldn't marry her. She said she did it, she had the gun, but they're still having a trial."

"She's going for an insanity plea, so she can get a reduced charge."

"Maybe she *was* crazy." Devon shook his head. "Sleeping with the father and the son."

"The popcorn is ready." Romare opened the machine's door and the aroma of fresh popcorn escaped into the air.

Everyone gathered around the machine, filling up their bowls with popcorn.

"I have an announcement to make," Steele said.

Tangi tilted her head to make eye contact with him. She had no idea what Steele was going to say.

Everyone stared at Steele, some munching on popcorn, some just curious.

"I want everyone in this room to know that I love Tangi very much," Steele said.

"I love you, too." Tangi melted within the warmth of his embrace, her eyes welling with tears.

A moment of silence passed, then Nolan said, "But Auntie Tangi, we already know that."

The alarm sounded at 6:30 A.M., waking Tangi and Steele up to an urban contemporary radio station. They almost drifted back to sleep, but the sounds of a hard-driving, hip-hop beat drew them back to consciousness.

"It's too early for that," Steele grumbled sleepily.

"Way too early."

Neither moved to turn the radio off.

"This next song is the latest from Cricket. It's going to be a hit big. You know how Cricket's songs blow up," said the radio dee-jay. "Rumor has it, the song was inspired by supermodel Tangi Ellington, host of VH5's new fashion show."

"Tangi did you hear that?"

Tangi sat up. "I hope he doesn't say anything bad about me," she said in a groggy voice.

"Sounds like an old Ohio Players song," Steele said, turning up the volume. "Yeah, sweet sticky thing."

Fully awake, they closely listened to the song's lyrics:

Met this model chick
A sweet girl, not a witch
So sexy and fine
She blew my mind

She's a sweet sticky thing
I'm gonna sting

She's the best thing yet
Place a thousand dollar bet
She will be mine
At the right time

She's a sweet sticky thing
I'm gonna sting

"You want me to sue him?" Steele asked when the song ended.

"He didn't say my name, so let's just not go there." She cuddled into his arms. "I like the part about the best thing yet. Because that's what you are to me. "

"Come here, you sweet sticky thing." He kissed her softly on the lips. *"My* sweet sticky thing."

Dear Readers:

I introduced Tangi Ellington in my book *The Promise*. Many of you wrote to me wanting to know what happened to Romare Ellington's little sister who couldn't wait to graduate from high school and pursue her dream to become a model.

She certainly fulfilled her dreams, didn't she? She achieved more than she imagined—fame, fortune, superstar success. Everything but love. But she discovered love the best way—by just being herself.

While she found love with Steele McDeal, it was heartwarming to show that Gillian and Romare's love was stronger than ever. Developing Devon's character was fun and interesting because of the kind of man he became.

What I like most about *The Promise* and *The Best Thing Yet* is the deep love and strong bond between the characters.

This is my fifth book, and I love getting reader letters just as much as when I opened my first fan letter about *Breeze*. So, please write me and let me know what you think of *The Best Thing Yet*. E-mail at ROB2ALLEN@AOL.COM or send a letter to P.O. Box 673634, Marietta, GA 30006. Please include a self-addressed stamped envelope for a quick reply. I can't wait to hear from you!

Love, peace, and happiness,
Robin Hampton Allen

About the Author

Robin Hampton Allen is an author, writer, and playwright. She is the author of five novels: *The Best Thing Yet, If I Were Your Woman, The Promise, Hidden Memories,* and *Breeze.* She has written articles for various publications: *Atlanta Woman, Black Elegance, Belle, Today's Black Woman* and *Diversity Careers.* An Atlanta-based theatre company produced her play, *The Bridal Shower.*

In 2002, Ms. Allen was included in Women Looking Ahead 100s List of Georgia's Most Powerful & Influential Women – Arts & Entertainment. She has extensive experience in marketing communications and public relations in the high-tech industry.

Ms. Allen grew up in Pittsburgh, Pennsylvania, and graduated from the University of Pittsburgh. She lives in Atlanta, Georgia, with her two daughters.

DO YOU KNOW AN ARABESQUE MAN?

CHARLES HORTON, JR.
ARABESQUE MAN 2002
featured on the cover of
One Sure Thing by Celeste O. Norfleet / Published Sept. 2003

Arabesque Man 2001 — PAUL HANEY
Holding Out for a Hero by Deirdre Savoy / Published Sept 2002

Arabesque Man 2000 — EDMAN REID
Love Lessons by Leslie Esdaile / Published Sept 2001

Arabesque Man 1999 — HAROLD JACKSON
Endless Love by Carmen Green / Published Sept 2000

WILL YOUR "ARABESQUE" MAN BE NEXT?

ONE GRAND PRIZE WINNER WILL WIN:
- 2 Day Trip to New York City
- Professional NYC Photo Shoot
- Picture on the Cover of an Arabesque Romance Novel
- Prize Pack & Profile on Arabesque Website and Newsletter
- $250.00

YOU WIN TOO!
- The Nominator of the Grand Prize Winner Receives a Prize Pack & Profile on Arabesque Website
- $250.00

To Enter: Simply complete the following items to enter your "Arabesque Man": (1) Compose an original essay that describes in 75 words or less why you think your nominee should win. (2) Include two recent photographs of him (head shot and one full length shot). Write the following information for both you and your nominee on the back of each photo: name, address, telephone number and the nominee's age, height, weight, and clothing sizes. (3) Include signature and date of nominee granting permission to nominator to enter photographs in contest. (4) Include a proof of purchase from an Arabesque romance novel—write the book title, author, ISBN number, and purchase location and price on a 3-1/2 x 5" card. (5) Entrants should keep a copy of all submissions. Submissions will not be returned and will be destroyed after the judging.

ARABESQUE regrets that no return or acknowledgment of receipt can be made because of the anticipated volume of responses. Arabesque is not responsible for late, lost, incomplete, inaccurate or misdirected entries. The Grand Prize Trip includes round trip transportation from a major airport nearest the winner's home, 2-day (1-night) hotel accommodations and ground transportation between the airport, hotel and Arabesque offices in New York. The Grand Prize Winner will be required to sign and return an affidavit of eligibility and publicity and liability release in order to receive the prize. The Grand Prize Winner will receive no additional compensation for the use of his image on an Arabesque novel, Website, or for any other promotional purpose. The entries will be judged by a panel of BET Arabesque personnel whose decisions regarding the winner and all other matters pertaining to the Contest are final and binding. By entering this Contest, entrants agree to comply with all rules and regulations. Contest ends October 31, 2003. Entries must be postmarked by October 31, 2003, and received no later than November 6, 2003.

SEND ENTRIES TO: The Arabesque Man Cover Model Contest, BET Books, One BET Plaza, 1235 W Street, NE, Washington, DC 20018. Open to legal residents of the U.S., 21 years of age or older. Illegible entries will be disqualified. Limit one entry per envelope. Odds of winning depend, in part, on the number of entries received. Void in Puerto Rico and where prohibited by law.

ARABESQUE

★BET BOOKS